First published in Great Britain in 2008 by Comma Press
www.commapress.co.uk

First published in Reykjavik as *Steintré* by Mál og menning, 2003.

A CIP catalogue record of this book is available from the British Library.

ISBN 1905583087
ISBN-13 978 1905583089

With the support of the Culture Programme (2007-2013) of the European Union.

Education and Culture DG
Culture Programme
Culture

This project has been funded with support from the European Commission.
This publication reflects the views only of the author, and the Commission
cannot be held responsible for any use which may be made of the information
contained therein.

The publisher gratefully acknowledges assistance from the Arts Council England
North West.

Set in Bembo 11/13 by David Eckersall
Printed and bound in England by SRP Ltd, Exeter

STONE TREE

by
Gyrðir Elíasson

Translated from the Icelandic by
Victoria Cribb

Contents

The Bus

The children darted back and forth around the old bus in the sunshine. I counted seven of them as I walked by, all ruddy-cheeked and noisy, in spite of their shabby clothes. The bus stood not on wheels but on wooden trestles, in a patch of rough grass amidst all the smart holiday homes. Most of its paint had flaked away and the windscreen was cracked. The exhaust pipe ran up to the roof where it had been converted into a chimney for an oil range. It smoked in the July breeze. A short way from the bus stood a rusty iron post. Several lengths of green nylon twine had been strung between this post and the bus, forming a line from which colourful washing flapped.

A woman appeared on the step of the bus, like a weary conductress, and called to the band of children: 'Lunchtime!' The children all piled in through the door as if it was a school bus come to take them home after a long, dull day in the classroom. Down on the rough ground, a man with a sledgehammer was driving in fence-posts. He was a lean figure in light-blue overalls, and from a distance bore more than a passing resemblance to Woody Guthrie. Perhaps he owned a guitar too. The woman appeared at the door once more, looking even wearier, and called again: 'Lunch!' The man looked up, laid down the sledgehammer among the tussocks and slowly made his way up to the old bus. From time to time he darted a glance at the smart holiday homes on either hand, with their hot tubs and oiled decking. When

1

he noticed me standing there on the road, watching him as if in a reverie, he raised a hand and waved. I came to my senses and waved back. He climbed into the bus, sat down behind the steering wheel, which was still in place, took out a cigarette and lit up. The woman came and laid her hand on his shoulder. It looked for all the world as if they were about to set off on a journey in their wheel-less bus, perhaps a circuit of the country. Smoke was still pouring from the pipe. The washing continued to flap in a riot of colour, almost touching the grass. The sun gleamed on the cracked windscreen.

I wonder what they're having for lunch, I thought, and how on earth seven children can sleep in there? I continued on my way, skirting a small copse where one of the luxury holiday homes stood on a shady lawn among the trees, then descended the hill, my eyes on the lofty mountain on the other side of the fjord, and finally reached the cabin where I was staying. It was a green hut, hardly any bigger than the bus, with red window frames and a few straggling trees around it. I was staying there alone, had been for a long time. Those seven children and their parents were the closest I had come to company for weeks. I was supposed to be thinking out my life afresh; if not for others, at least for myself.

Once I had entered the cabin, I lay down on a short couch in the corner, against the wooden wall. Freud had been my first thought when I saw the couch. It had a psychoanalytical look, though in practice I tended not to spend any time cogitating when I lay on it. I simply fell asleep, as I did now, on that sunny summer's day. I pulled the curtain across the window to dim the brightness, curled up on the couch and dozed off.

I dreamed of the bus. It came careering down the slope, now sporting big, gleaming tyres and newly polished hubcaps. Its bodywork had been painted jet black. It charged onwards in a cloud of dust. The windows were no longer cracked but tinted so that no one could see in. Then one of them was

2

wound down and fourteen small hands reached out towards me; fourteen small hands, like the petals of a flower. After that, the black bus drove away down the road, over the cattle grid, to disappear beyond the grey gravel flats. I thought it odd that the bus should be dragging the rusty post behind it, with all the rainbow-coloured washing bellying and tumbling in a cloud of dust, like an ominous long-tailed kite trying to take to the air.

It was half past five when I awoke. I had slept for several hours and felt hungry. Rising from the psychoanalyst's couch, I looked out of the window. I was almost surprised to see the bus still in place higher up the slope, with its flaking paint. I saw the children charging around it as before, and the man out on the waste-ground again, banging in posts. Some cows from the farm down by the river were grazing in the nearby meadow, and now the children could be seen heading in single file towards the herd.

After a while I went to prepare myself a snack, and switched on the radio. The news reported that a bus full of children on their way to summer camp had driven off the main west road out of Reykjavík. The cause of the accident was unclear but the newsreader mentioned, for some reason, that the bus was black. My eyes flew to the couch in the corner.

A House of Two Stories

That winter we lived on the outskirts of the village. A narrow road ran along the seashore, then there was a small bridge over the river, and beyond that the jetty and co-op. Sometimes in the mornings before my wife and child were awake, I would go out and walk down to the end of the jetty where I would stare out to sea as if waiting for a ship to take me away. I held an invisible suitcase in my hand. But coasters found it hard to put in here; on the rare occasions they did, they seemed almost to fill the fjord, which was not large.

From time to time I would encounter one of the teachers from the primary school on my morning walks. He had been here several years, a quiet, steady type, usually dressed in a brown overcoat, peaked cap and thick glasses. I always had the impression he would have been more at home on the streets of Reykjavík than here, on the bleak, narrow gravel path along the seashore. This teacher lived on the ground floor of a two-storey house that stood one further out from ours. The floor above was occupied by a vicar and his wife. The vicar was a modest chap who did not require a special vicarage and had asked permission instead to live on the top floor of this house because it afforded a good view of the sea.

The vicar and teacher seemingly had nothing to do with one another, yet I'd heard that they had once long ago been drinking partners in Reykjavík. Both had now given up the bottle. Their living arrangement was not otherwise noteworthy, except in one detail. They both translated books, and that particular winter it so happened, oddly enough, that both were translating works by the same author. Not, however, the same book. One was working on his longest work, the other on his shortest. The author in question was John Steinbeck. The vicar sat in the upstairs flat, toiling away every day on his translation of *East of Eden*. The teacher, meanwhile, sat in his den in the evenings, translating *The Pearl*. As a matter of fact, he had already translated it once before, but perhaps he was dissatisfied with his earlier attempt.

The villagers soon caught wind of these endeavours. Nothing escapes people's attention in a small place like this. All the houses had names, and theirs was soon rechristened 'Steinbekkur'. As a Steinbeck fan, I was rather curious about their progress and keen to read *East of Eden* in Icelandic, although I had read it twice in the original as well as *Journal of a Novel*, the diary he wrote during its composition. I'd read the latter so often that my copy fell apart – it was only a badly glued paperback – so I ordered another. I had also read *The Pearl* in the older translation, and thought the teacher might be right about the need for a new version.

As I returned from the jetty early in the morning, still with the invisible suitcase in my hand, I would, as I said, sometimes meet the teacher on his way to school; brown overcoat buttoned up to his neck, peaked cap pulled down over his glasses, as he strode along with a purposeful set to his shoulders. I always said good morning but he rarely replied. At best I'd hear him mutter something. I was dying to ask him about *The Pearl*, find out how he was getting on, talk to him generally about Steinbeck, but he always stalked past, never giving me an opening. In late afternoon he could be seen coming back the same way, which was the only way. In between those times one didn't see him out at all, only the light in his den of an evening. I used to see his silhouette at the desk, his head wreathed in smoke, reminding me of an old film noir. Meanwhile all the lights blazed on the floor above.

I didn't know the vicar well either. Of course, he had christened our child when we moved here, but that was more or less it. He was no less reserved than the teacher and kept to his house for the most part. I could understand that in the circumstances: *East of Eden* was a long book and tricky to translate. Somehow that winter it hardly struck us as strange that in one and the same house in a village by the Arctic Ocean two men should be busy translating works by the same American author. In fact, it's not until now, as I write this, that I realise it *was* a bit unusual.

Spring arrived late and cold. Snow lay in the hayfields well into May. At some point during those cold spring days the news spread around the village that the vicar had finished *East of Eden* and sent the manuscript south to his publisher. At around the same time, the day after school broke up, the teacher headed south to Reykjavík as well. Several days later it was announced that he would be reading his translation of *The Pearl* on the radio. And so the translators' odd cohabitation ended. The teacher did not return in the autumn, and the vicar seemed to have had enough of the sea view, since he and his wife now moved to a little house just above the co-op. Given their initial satisfaction with the other house, I couldn't help thinking that the vicar must have felt lonely when the other translator left, even though they had barely exchanged a word. After all, there must have been some sort of mysterious bond between them, almost a secret brotherhood – surely?

I listened to the entire serialisation of *The Pearl* on the radio. The teacher read very well, accustomed as he was to doing so for children, which makes for the best readers. His translation was never published but I'm still convinced it's better than the old one. *East of Eden* came out in two volumes early in the autumn. I bought the work directly from the translator as soon as it was published. This was just before he moved into the little house. He looked weary when I mounted the stairs to his flat and announced my business, but responded politely and invited me into his study with its piles of papers and books. He handed me the volumes, bound in brown leather. I asked him to sign them. He said that sort of thing was really only for the author, but reluctantly picked up a pen, scribbled something in the first volume and handed it to me. I opened it and read:

On behalf of Steinbeck.

Underneath he had written his own name. I thanked him and did not mention that I found this an odd sort of inscription. The vicar said nothing; he seemed distracted. His wife came in and offered me coffee, but I declined and went downstairs. When I looked back up at the landing, the vicar was still standing there, a thin, lined figure, in his white shirt and braces, now with a lit cigarette. He gave me a brief wave with the hand that held the glowing cigarette. The movement released a delicate cloud of blue smoke that put me in mind of Orthodox priests waving censers during mass. That was the last time I saw him. I went home and read late into the night.

We moved away shortly afterwards, before another winter set in.

Chain Reaction

1

It was dark in the room when I was woken by a peculiar noise. I sat up quickly and stared into the blackness, unable to remember where I was for a moment, as often happens when one is transported abruptly between worlds. Then I got my bearings. I was at the writer's retreat in Hveragerdi. It was night, in the middle of February, and I had lived there alone for three weeks now. I had informed everyone that I was going there to write, and discouraged visitors, but the days had passed one after another without my writing so much as a word. My time had been spent on other things, such as peering into the floodlit greenhouses in the dusk; watching jungle plants spreading their leaves on the other side of the clear glass while the frost outside pierced one to the bone. It was an alternative sort of greenhouse effect.

I had been dreaming that I was in a diving bell, sinking deeper and deeper into a pitch-black sea, with a dim light shining in the chamber. A shark appeared at the porthole and snapped at me so violently that I could hear its teeth grinding against the metal and thick glass.

What could have caused the noise that had woken me? It had sounded like a sort of scraping sound, coming either from the sitting room or upstairs in the loft. It could hardly be burglars in a quiet village like this. I got hesitantly out of bed. The floor was cold; the radiator in my room wasn't working properly. I put on my dressing gown, turned on the light and went out. All was quiet. Several books lay on the sitting-room table, some of them open. The ceiling light buzzed strangely, as if a fly was trapped in the shade, yet the season for flies was over. My gaze fell on the window where the darkness pressed up against the glass. Was I still in the diving bell – trapped in my dream?

I heard the sound again. It *was* a scraping noise from upstairs, as if an iron chain were being dragged slowly and jerkily along the floorboards. The loft was closed; the trapdoor was down and had not been touched since I came to the house. It was only a storage loft, and the tiny window in the gable end was always tightly closed. Yet now I heard a heavy tread on the floor upstairs, back and forth, and the simultaneous dragging of the chain.

Looking up, I saw drops of water swelling from the ceiling. One by one they began to fall, first on my face, then on my books, laptop, the little television with the indoor aerial and the worn floorboards. I went over to the gable window and looked out, and immediately sensed someone going to the little window in the gable directly above. The night was bright with stars and freezing cold; there was rime on the windowpanes and inside the glass too, as it was only single-glazed. I scratched absent-mindedly at the frost pattern with my finger, drawing the leaf of some plant I had seen in the greenhouses.

The ceiling was still dripping when I turned away from the window. I went to the laptop and ran my hand over it and my palm came away wet. Under the lid was the keyboard that I had barely touched during these three weeks. The footsteps started again upstairs and the chain was jerked with more force than before. My eyes went to the trapdoor. I headed into the bedroom and fetched my clothes from the chair. The clock showed 3:35. I dressed hastily and went out again, grabbing an open book from the table. It was a recent biography of Houdini, an American pocket book. I put on my anorak and woolly hat, zipped the book into my pocket, and stepped outside, closing the door behind me. I tested the door; it was locked. Only now did I remember that the keys were inside.

I saw the Pleiades directly above the leafless sycamore. But my sight was deteriorating and these days I could barely make out four of the cluster of stars that I had always found so entrancing when I was small and used to lie awake, gazing slantwise out of my bedroom window.

2

On the other side of the road was a small stand of trees, mostly conifers. They were black in the gloom and increased my sense of dread. Yet I walked towards them, and entering a narrow path, followed it down to the river. The waterfall was almost entirely fettered in ice, though a little water trickled over the rocks in the middle. A small cave had formed in the ice wall, like the one where Merlin had sat after losing his powers. The plunge pool was frozen too, leaving only a hole in the ice where the trickle of water fell. There was a wooden bench on the brink. I sat down and peered into the ice cave. On the hill across the river an enormous, snow-white building stood in total darkness, with a convex skylight that could have been an observatory. The woman in the shop had told me that it was a luxury hotel, intended for rich celebrities, and that the rooms contained all sorts of extraordinary fittings to cater for their whims. That may have been right, though I had never seen a light in any of the windows in the evenings, nor any sign of life in the day. But of course that could be evidence of the guests' Californian eccentricity.

I began to muse on how I had woken, the scraping of the chain and the thudding of wet boots and the unused laptop on the table and all the drops of water and my dream about the depths of the ocean and the pool here under the ice and the waterfall that hardly dripped and the Pleiades that had lost three stars in just over thirty years. I fumbled for Houdini's biography in my pocket. Then I thought of a woman I had once known, who was no longer part of my life. Suddenly a light went on in the roof window of the hotel to the stars.

Book After Book

He stood by the window, staring out into the drizzle. Then turned and glanced around the flat with absent gaze, as if he were only a visitor there. Boxes from Amazon were strewn all over the place, and new books littered the tables and chairs. Struck by a sudden idea, he went over to the fridge and opened it.

The fridge was half full of books but contained almost nothing to eat. He grabbed one of the books, a recent complete edition of Vitezslav Nezval's poems in English, and leafed through it for a while. Then he replaced the book beside a lone milk carton and closed the fridge. Next he stooped to the oven and opened the door. Piles of books lay on the oven shelf, including an eight-volume edition of *Don Quixote* in Icelandic, and a biography of the American poet Delmore Schwartz. He grabbed the biography, flicked through it and sighed as he recalled the drunkenness and suffering on its pages. He quickly replaced it on the oven shelf. Next he went into the hall, past sagging shelves bearing double-banked rows of books. On the windowsill at the end of the hall high stacks of magazines almost blocked out the grey daylight.

He went into the bathroom and urinated with low moans. Then turned to the bathroom cabinet and opened it. The cabinet contained a number of books and some bottles of pills. These included a biography of Strindberg by Olof Lagercrantz, all Carson McCullers' stories in a single volume, a small bottle of 5 mg diazepam tablets and several volumes of Icelandic poetry. He picked one out at random.

> *We two, the night*
> *all this, all that*

Replacing the book, he locked the cabinet, moved from the bathroom to the bedroom and lit a cigarette. The windowsill was completely buried in books. Against the wall opposite the bed stood a large bookcase, crammed to bursting. The bedside table carried a great pile of all kinds of literature: a jumble of folklore, modern French poetry, Icelandic novels and foreign travel books. On top of the pile lay a large copper ashtray which looked as if it might topple off at any minute. He sat down on the bed and smoked the cigarette halfway down, before placing it in the ashtray where it slowly smouldered away.

He noticed that it had rained in through the top window during last night's storm and Orwell's collected works had become warped by moisture on the windowsill. He put the book on the hot radiator to dry, with a newspaper underneath.

The phone rang. It was a friend of his who had been bowled over by Henrik Nordbrandt's new volume of poems. They discussed the fact for some time. He lay down on the bed while he talked. Finally he managed to convince the caller that Nordbrandt's book was not so very remarkable after all. This required quite an effort on his part and he was worn out when he replaced the receiver.

He closed his eyes and tried not to think, but books hovered like sinister birds in his imagination, flapping their black covers, ruffling their white pages like breast-feathers. He managed to ward off this image, but now lines of poetry began to seep into his thoughts, some no better than the ones he had read beside the bathroom cabinet.

Giving up on sleep, he extracted *The Story of My*

Thinking by the old Icelandic philosopher Brynjúlfur of Minni-Núpur from under the ashtray and commenced reading in the middle. He read for about half an hour. Then the doorbell rang. He couldn't be bothered to get up and carried on reading. It rang again. Finally he got up and walked slowly to the door. The cupboard in the entrance hall was half open, revealing a glimpse of rows of books.

By the time he opened the front door, there was nobody there. Leaning against the doorpost he stared at the wet, pallid-grey grass by the steps. It seemed impossible that this autumnal vegetation would ever be green again.

After some thought, he took out a raincoat that hung in the hall cupboard among the books. He buttoned up the coat, stuck several paperbacks in his pockets, laced up his shoes and went out. Rounding the corner of the house, he strolled past the sports field and lit a cigarette, sheltering it from the drizzle. The sky was as grey as over a coal-mining village in Wales. He met no one. Before long he had pulled a book out of his pocket and begun to read as he walked, the cigarette dangling from the corner of his mouth. The pages grew gradually damp, and he turned them with care.

To Hear a Pencil Fall

The sky threatened rain as we pulled into the drive in front of the guesthouse. I got out and looked around. The house stood at the top of a grassy slope, commanding a panoramic view of the green valley with its tracery of blue rivers. The mountains looked strangely jagged, as if newly created.

The house could have done with a coat of paint. Above the door hung an old sign that read 'GUESTHOUSE EINISBREKKA'. The pane of glass in the front door was cracked. Several cars were parked outside, dusty from the long drive.

'I don't like it,' my wife said.

'Come on,' I said casually. 'It's bound to be okay.'

I went inside and came face to face with an odd-looking, middle-aged man with a pencil behind his ear. He said he had one vacancy.

'Number nine,' he said, taking the pencil and writing the number in the air, before sticking it behind his ear again.

'Thank you,' I replied, and went back outside. 'There's a room free,' I told my wife.

'Oh, shouldn't we go somewhere else?' she asked.

'I don't feel like going any further today,' I said wearily. She gave in, and we fetched our bags and carried them inside. This time I noticed an oddly bitter smell in the hall that I hadn't been aware of before – unless it hadn't been present?

'What's that smell?' my wife whispered.

'Haven't a clue,' I replied in a low voice.

The man with the pencil emerged from a back room and handed us a key attached with an elastic band to a label on which the number 9 had been written – in pencil. We found our room and opened the door. It contained two extremely narrow beds, divided by a little table on which stood an ancient portable radio. There were threadbare curtains drawn across the window, and an extraordinarily flowery carpet, frayed at the threshold. The bedcovers had a disagreeably swirly design.

'I want to change my mind,' my wife said.

'Out of the question,' I replied, plonking myself down on the bed. It creaked. I can't say I was surprised. The bathroom, which was a bit squalid, was down the corridor, and it was possible to take a shower there as well. When I went along to use it, I again noticed that acrid smell in the corridor, somehow suggestive of burnt almonds; not that I was even sure I'd ever smelt burnt almonds.

It was nearing suppertime, so we went out to the dining room that was built sunroom-style and housed in an annex to the original house. One wall was made of glass and offered a view of the whole valley. Once again I found myself fascinated by the tracery of rivers on the gravel beds far below, like bony, twisted fingers.

The dining room was empty apart from a foreign couple who were munching something from a cool-box that stood beside their table. We had a cool-box too and brought out this and that to put on our own table. The foreign couple whispered to each other in low voices and we couldn't make out a word, but I thought they were speaking English and somehow got the impression they were American.

The man with the pencil behind his ear poked his head briefly into the dining room and nodded to us before disappearing. It was strangely quiet in the house, as if there was no one in all those rooms that were supposedly occupied. But what about those cars outside? It was too early in the evening for everyone to have gone to bed.

'There's something uncannily mysterious about this house,' my wife said as she buttered herself a slice of bread.

'I don't see why life shouldn't contain a healthy amount of mystery,' I said, perhaps coming across as a little superior.

'Yes, a *healthy* amount,' she said, stressing the word.

'Is that the smell of burnt almonds?' I asked her, sniffing the air.

'I don't know,' she said. 'But if it is almonds, they must have been mouldy. And anyway, who can have been toasting almonds here?'

I glanced at the American couple, but they didn't look the type to have been toasting almonds in the little kitchen in the corner.

'I'm having an early night,' my wife announced, rising shortly afterwards. We returned to our room, and then she went out again and I heard her turning on the shower in the bathroom. Sound carried through the paper-thin walls, yet I couldn't hear any other signs of life in the house, except the occasional heavy footfall in the corridor. I had the feeling it was the owner.

My wife returned from her shower. She was in her dressing gown and looked rather fetching. I was about to hint as much to her when she said she was very tired. Taking off her dressing gown, she crawled naked into bed, turned to face the wall and said good night. Biting my lip, I wished her good night in return, but it didn't exactly sound heartfelt.

I wanted to turn on the radio but decided against it. Instead I reached into my bag and pulled out *The Strange Case of Dr Jekyll and Mr Hyde*. Actually, I had read the book before but was now reading it again. It was just light enough in the room on that July night to read without switching on the lamp. Judging by the sound, my wife was asleep.

I was plunged at once into the sinister, rainy streets of London. But all of a sudden I heard a strange noise from the room next door. An oddly muffled sound. At first I thought it was the sound of people having sex and strained my ears, curiosity getting the better of me. Then I heard distinctly that it was the sound of weeping; muffled, painful weeping. Somebody was crying into their pillow. It wasn't a child, I was sure it was an adult. For a moment I toyed with the idea of waking my wife and asking her opinion, but decided against it. I returned to London, transporting myself more than a century back in time.

I had read much of the book by the time I fell asleep. By then the weeping had long since ceased, and I'd heard the man with the pencil walk past repeatedly. And because the walls were so thin, I thought I heard the pencil fall onto the worn carpet in the corridor. I pictured him bending, grumpily picking it up and replacing it behind his ear.

I tossed and turned and my bed creaked absurdly, but at last I nodded off. I dreamed of a room with a fire burning in the hearth and the shadowy figure of a man who would have been perfectly at home in Stevenson's world. The man threw a handful of something onto the fire and I thought I could smell that acrid odour in my dream; the odour of burnt almonds.

Some time in the middle of the night I awoke abruptly, needing a pee. I went out into the corridor, which was gloomier than I had expected. I could hear no sounds of movement, nothing at all. But when I returned to our room I heard the sound of muffled weeping again from next door. Instead of getting into my own bed, I squeezed in beside my wife. She lay hot and naked against the wall, but didn't stir and I didn't try to wake her, just lay and stared up at the cracks in the ceiling with its old-fashioned light fitting hanging down. Nothing could be heard from the floor above.

We woke up fairly late next morning. The daylight entering through the window was grey. We ate breakfast in the sunroom, with the rain streaming down the glass. The mountains were invisible, shrouded in fog. No one else was breakfasting. I looked out into the drive and saw that only one car remained besides our own.

The man with the pencil appeared at the door of the sunroom. I beckoned to him and he stumped over to us. I pointed out that we still had to settle up, and he went into the back room next door, returning with the bill. Although the amount seemed a bit steep, I didn't comment on the fact. I paid in cash and he stuffed the notes into his shirt pocket.

'We should make a move,' my wife said. I could tell she was uncomfortable. We got ready to leave and shortly afterwards were on our way, the rain rattling on the windows of the car, windscreen wipers working away frantically. The dirt road had turned into a quagmire. I glanced in the rear-view mirror and watched the house recede.

★

About a month later I read in the paper that GUESTHOUSE EINISBREKKA had burnt to the ground.

'Doesn't surprise me,' my wife said, sounding almost pleased. 'He was probably toasting almonds; maybe he deliberately forgot them in the pan.'

I nodded. It didn't really come as a surprise to me either. I imagined the yellow pencil lying on the worn carpet as it went up in flames.

This summer we returned to those parts, from sheer curiosity, of course. A bleak scene met us when I pulled into the drive. The house had completely vanished and soil had been spread over the foundations. But lower down the slope a single sheet of corrugated iron from the roof lay black and scorched in the grass.

The Silver Nose

He sat by the window, gazing up at the starry sky. Beside him on the table lay the silver nose. He picked up a heavy tome from beside the nose and began to leaf through it, turning the pages slowly and carefully as he peered at them in the dim light of the candle. Every now and then he would look up and crane his neck into the window embrasure. The cat lay sleeping at his feet. It was a fat old tabby with a shaggy coat that could be used to warm one's toes. The very thought of the icy winter made the astronomer indignant that he, Tycho Brahe, should have to endure such a bitterly cold house.

The book was about the movements of the celestial bodies. He poured a glass of wine from a leather flask and sipped as he read. Before long he heard somebody at the door. It was very late and his wife had gone to bed. Putting down the book, he rose reluctantly to his feet and went to the door, drawing back the bolt. Outside stood a man in a black cowl, with the hood over his head. He stooped, and his face could not be seen.

'Good evening,' he said. There was a remote quality to his voice that put Tycho in mind of a faint star in the black void. He returned the greeting.

'Is there any chance of lodging for the night?'

The astronomer thought for a moment. His wife was not keen on company. He would have consulted her but she had gone to sleep and would not be best pleased in the morning to find a visitor had spent the night in the house.

'I'm afraid you'll have to look elsewhere,' he said.

The stranger straightened up, pushing the cowl back on his head, and stared into Tycho's face with the piercing, yellow-grey eyes of a lizard. His lips were pursed; implacable hatred informed every feature. Tycho looked away, brushing a flustered hand over his face. He felt the dip where his nose should have been.

'This will cost you dear,' the cowled man said, flinging the hood over his face again and turning his back on Tycho. It was as if the darkness had assumed human form. Tycho closed the door, went over to the table and sat down on the hard wooden chair. He picked up his wineglass and took a sip, then carefully stuck on his silver nose with yellow gum, before reaching for his book and leaning towards the candle to see better. The nose glittered in the glow like a fallen star.

★

He read at the table for a while, then reached for his writing things and embarked on the letter to Prague that he had meant to finish long ago. Perhaps it was too late now. He darted a glance at the inkstand; its black contents reminded him of the cowl. It was so cold here that the ink almost froze. The cat slept on at his feet.

The Piano

That afternoon two removals men came round and manoeuvred it with ropes and pulley through the door and into the living room. The boy watched in silence. He did not want this instrument.

'You must learn to play the piano,' his father had said one evening, with a determined set to his face. The boy's eyes went to his mother but she only nodded. He had gone up to his room and stared out of the window at the leafless tree.

The removals men took the ropes and pulley and walked back down the steps to the blue van. They started the engine and grey diesel fumes dispersed in the chill autumn air. The boy shut the door, went back into the living room and stared at the alien object. He did not want to go too close or to touch it, yet he couldn't help privately admiring the black sheen of the wood.

His father came home from work towards evening. He wanted to start the lessons straight after supper. They went over to the piano and sat down side by side. The boy did as he was told, hating every note. His mother appeared in the doorway and smiled as she watched father and son in the glow of the lamp. He did not look at her.

After a while his father stood up and ran a careful hand over the piano. Then he sat down in front of the television and forgot about the boy, who went upstairs and put on his pyjamas, brushed his teeth and climbed into bed. He needed to get an early night because it was school tomorrow.

Switching on the lamp by his bed, he picked up the book that lay on the bedside table. It was a big picture book about Harley Davidsons. He pored over the pictures until his mother came to the door and said: 'It'll be fun to learn the piano, don't you think? Your father can teach you a little to start with, because he once had lessons himself, then you can go to the music school.'

He nodded and closed the book. She came over and kissed him, then switched off the light and left the room. He lay awake in the darkness for a long time, fantasising about a Harley Davidson on an American freeway. In his mind he was wearing a green-tinted helmet, roaring along the road at the head of a big motorcycle gang, all clad in leathers.

Time passed but he could not get to sleep. He looked at the clock that ticked with a neon-yellow hand on the chest of drawers. It was just past midnight. Getting out of bed, he cautiously opened the door to the landing. All the lights were out. They had gone to bed.

He descended the dark stairs in his pyjamas. The steps were carpeted and did not creak. A peculiar silence reigned in the house; to him it felt deeper than ever before. Perhaps it had deepened since the instrument entered the house.

He walked barefoot into the laundry, feeling the cold stone of the floor by the drain under his soles. His father's toolbox stood on a shelf in the corner. Opening the box, he rummaged in it quietly until he found what he was looking for. After that, he went into the living room where the black colossus stood. The only light was the faint illumination from a streetlight outside the window.

He sat down at the piano, lifted the lid and aimed the chisel, peering with intense concentration at the keyboard, then began nimbly to score scratches and grooves in the keys. He pressed the keys down with exaggerated care before scratching them, in an effort to ensure that they did not sound. Yet every now and then a low note rang out, like a muffled cry of pain. First he scratched letters and patterns on the white keys, then he started on the black ones, applying the chisel to the end of each one and prising off the top. Although he couldn't really see how he was getting on, it was fun and he soon became absorbed in his task. Now for the black case itself. He scratched his initials and those of his parents here and there, then scored a sun and a crescent moon in the darkness that is the origin of all creation.

His eyes became accustomed to the gloom. The chisel was as incisive as the human mind. He was just starting to carve out the lid when the light suddenly came on. Looking up, he dropped the chisel and it fell on the carpet with a dull thud.

The Tea Lights

The mountain had turned grey with snow when I looked out of the window that autumn morning. It was as if everything had changed; as if I had changed too and my thoughts had turned grey. Yet I had dreamed quite well, better than for a long time, with none of the nightmares that had plagued me recently. There had been little to do in the greenhouses for the past few weeks, and I had not worked for several days. When I started working there, years ago, I sometimes came home with flowers. But I had given that up long ago.

I let the curtain fall and looked at the bed. She was still asleep, the duvet pulled up over her head. Putting on my dressing gown, I went downstairs and into the bathroom for a leak. Then I went into the kitchen, took down a box of cereal from the shelf and turned on the coffee maker. When I opened the cereal I noticed that it was months past its sell-by date. After I had eaten breakfast and read the paper, I went into the sitting room, sat down by the window and stared out. The greenhouses were clearly visible between the trees. The phone rang. It was Mum. I could tell at once from her voice that something had happened.

'Is it Dad?' I asked.

'Yes,' she said.

'When?'

'Some time last night.'

'I'm on my way,' I said and ended the conversation. I ran upstairs. She was still asleep. I prodded her.

'What?' she mumbled.

'It's Dad,' I said.

She sat up. I told her I would take the bus later. I half hoped she'd say she wanted to come with me, but she didn't. And I didn't ask her to. We had long ago given up talking to one another.

Before leaving, I grabbed a book from the shelf to read on the bus, just in case I found myself able to focus on something other than what had happened. As I opened the door the hinges emitted a strange shrill whine, like the sound of weeping.

two

I couldn't read on the bus journey over the mountain. I just sat among the other passengers, staring out of the window. There was a teenage boy in the seat in front of me, with a small black kitten in a half-unzipped sports bag. The kitten poked its head through the opening and mewed pathetically. The driver darted a glance in the rear-view mirror from time to time, clearly disgruntled at having to ferry pets from place to place.

I was thinking about Dad. About the time he bought his first car and I was allowed to go for a drive with him. They still drove on the left in those days but signs had been set up along the road, advertising the imminent change to the right. He was sometimes ahead of his times, and during these jaunts in the car he had a tendency to veer over into the right-hand lane until we saw cars coming towards us, honking their horns, and he was forced to swerve sharply to the left. I also remembered the time he came home from abroad with a Meccano set and we spent a whole evening trying in vain to assemble something from the bits. Dad cursed and swore. The box was never taken out again.

The bus crawled up to the central bus station. I got out, walked through the terminal building and took a taxi from outside the main entrance. The taxi driver was middle-aged and overweight, with dandruff and a habit of clearing his throat. He chewed Victory pastilles the whole time and once even offered the packet to me. I declined.

The city looked autumnal: the leaves had begun to fall from the trees; the first storms had been and gone. The driver drove to the house where Mum now lived alone. The meter ticked, its digital numbers unnervingly reminiscent of a hospital cardiograph. The trees in the garden seemed strangely sparse now, the plants withered; so different from the greenhouses at home where nothing was allowed to decay. A torn page from the morning paper lay in the road in front of Dad's car. From experience I was fairly sure it was the obituaries. When a page of the newspaper is found on the street it is almost invariably from the obituary section. I don't know why. Perhaps they use lighter paper in that section. Or people are so afraid of death that they jettison those pages straight away.

I paid the taxi driver, and he offered me the cough sweets again in parting. This time I accepted one and walked up the concrete path chewing vigorously, with that bittersweet flavour in my mouth.

three

I sat in the study upstairs, where Dad often used to sit reading. I could hear Mum moving about busily in the kitchen below. There was the clatter of a saucepan, or was it a waffle-iron? The shelves were full of books. All kinds of works rubbed shoulders there, from children's stories to philosophical tracts. My gaze was caught by one spine in particular: *Life and Death* by the philosopher Sigurdur Nordal. I reached for the book, but didn't take it down from the shelf. It wouldn't change anything. Somehow I couldn't feel anything. I was just there.

It was like before, yet somehow completely different.

That night, as I was lying under the white duvet in the bedroom next door, I suddenly had the illusion that the bedclothes were a shroud. I grabbed my phone from the dressing table and called my wife. For a moment I wasn't sure which was home – there or here. The phone rang several times. When she answered we said little, as usual. She asked how Mum was bearing up, and how I was doing. I said I didn't know, and asked in return how she was doing. She said it was the same with her. Our conversation didn't last much longer.

four

That night I couldn't sleep. I got dressed and walked quietly downstairs and out onto the steps, then down into the garden, wearing Dad's slippers. The night was starlit and cold. The grass had yellowed to the roots, and a few yellow leaves with black spots lay on the lawn, resembling nothing so much as sleepy cats' eyes in the glow of the outdoor light. It had never before occurred to me that leaves were shaped like eyes. Perhaps trees could see?

It felt good, walking on the grass in the slippers. They were soft and warm. I walked right round the garden, through the trees and down to the little concrete pond that was generally dry, as it was now. Suddenly it occurred to me to rectify this state of affairs. Picking up a hose that lay coiled by the house, I eased it onto the tap on the wall, turned the water on full and pulled the hose down to the edge of the pond. I listened to the gushing sound as I watched the water flow. Then turned and saw Mum standing on the steps in her dressing gown.

'What are you doing?' she asked.

'I'm going to float candles in it,' I said.

'I see,' she said with a shiver and retreated inside.

Gradually the stone basin filled with water.

A taxi cruised slowly along the road below, without stopping. I started thinking about the taxi driver who had driven me here, and tasted again the bitter flavour of the throat pastilles, my childhood favourite, to which I had once been incredibly addicted. They had given me a sensation of intense pleasure: I didn't know then that they contained Benzedrine. The sweets no longer have the same impact on one's mental state now that this fine ingredient has been removed.

The wind had picked up, rippling the water in the little pond. It might prove difficult to keep the tea lights burning. Perhaps they would sink to the bottom with a quiet hiss. I looked up at the sky. There were a few stars: remote, cold tea lights.

Bird Hunting

After the crack had faded and the bird had fallen from the bough onto the ground in the garden, the boy looked around, lowered the gun and walked towards the stone wall that separated the trees from the straggling grass of the farmyard.

He opened the gate of the garden; the little plot must surely have been the smallest flower garden in the world. Innumerable plants grew here in massed confusion in the oddly shaped beds. Under the crooked poplars, which struggled to survive the relentless northerly blast, the bird lay oozing blood. The boy put down his gun on the strip of grass beside the flowerbed and picked up the bird in his hand. It was still faintly warm.

The boy left his gun lying where it was and went out through the garden gate with the bird in his hand. He cast a brief glance at the mountains which towered sombrely on the other side of the fjord river. The hayfield running down to the river was pale green. He opened the door on the utility room side and went in.

His mother greeted him in the kitchen doorway. She looked tired, as usual.

'Have you been shooting again?' she asked. There was a note of defeat in her voice when she added: 'The birds ought to be protected in my garden.'

He slipped past her without answering. Grabbing a crumpled newspaper from the counter by the kitchen window, he carried it into the sitting room with the bird.

There he sat down at the worn wooden table, spread out the newspaper and laid the bird on it. The wound in its breast was still oozing. On the shelf above the couch in the corner was a book called *Birds of Iceland and Europe*. He got up to fetch it and returned to his seat at the table. He flicked back and forth through the book, poring and reading, glancing at the bird from time to time, then reading and turning the pages again. Finally he stopped at a colour illustration towards the middle of the book, labelled 'CHAFFINCH'. He read eagerly what it had to say about the species. It *was* a chaffinch. There was no doubt. He stroked a finger along its flank but as he did so a little of the bird's blood smeared the paper. He wiped it off with his shirtsleeve. Then he closed the book, and standing up again, took it to the shelf and replaced it beside the other books. His mother came to the door and watched him with an expression of half-suppressed disapproval.

'Why are you doing this?' she asked. 'You know what your father would have said.'

The boy did not answer her this time either. He went back to the table, wrapped the paper carefully round the bird and carried it past his mother. She made way reluctantly for boy and bird. He walked through the kitchen into the dim pantry. There were countless brown glass jars on the sagging shelves, and tins from which the paper had been torn off, so the metal gleamed faintly in the slender ray of light that fell through the narrow corner window above the centrifuge. The edges of the shelves were lined with strips of worn oilcloth decorated with an animal pattern, in which a fringe had been cut. The strips drooped down in some places where the drawing pins that were meant to keep them in place had fallen out.

The boy paused a moment in the gloom of the pantry and glanced at the shelves, inhaling the mingled smell of countless varieties of food and spices. Then he opened the huge old Westinghouse freezer.

At the top were a number of vagrant birds, all wrapped

in newspaper like the chaffinch. Icy heads and beaks glittered in the dim light that came on in the freezer when it was opened. The bulb was dying; the light flickered and at times faded completely, but the intermittent glow was enough to enable one to read the long-forgotten newspaper headlines, some several years old.

The boy arranged the bird's tepid body in its newspaper wrapping on top of the heap of its frozen kindred. Then he closed the lid slowly, like a funeral director closing a coffin for the last time.

When he returned to the bright kitchen his mother had started making waffles. She was standing at the stove, with the ancient, coal-black waffle-iron on the glowing hotplate. The smell of waffles spread through the room, raising the boy's spirits. He looked at his mother, but she did not return his look. As far as he could see, her face still wore the expression it always wore when he shot vagrant birds. 'You know what your father would have said,' echoed in his mind.

Returning to the sitting room, he took a pad of lined writing paper and a biro from a drawer in the teak cabinet, and sat down at the table again. He dated the sheet of paper at the top and began to write.

Dear Mr Finnur,

Today I shot a chaffinch. It was not badly damaged, just a wound on the breast, I put it in the freezer and will send it to you later like all the other birds I've told you about. One day the freezer will be full, but it's a Westinghouse so it's big.

Folding the sheet of paper, he put it in his shirt pocket, moved over to the couch in the corner and lay down, leaving the writing pad on the table with the pen beside it. He closed his eyes and breathed in the smell of waffles, listening to the sizzling as the mixture poured from the wooden spoon onto the iron. Then he remembered that the rifle was still lying out in the garden. It didn't matter, he could fetch it afterwards: it wouldn't rain now.

He reflected on what he had read about the chaffinch, and how it had sat all unsuspecting on the poplar branch, gripping its little claws into the bark and staring out into the air. He wondered what gave rise to its Icelandic name – 'book finch'. Was it because it looked like an open book when it raised its wings? He didn't know. Perhaps he should have included this question in his letter to the ornithologist.

'Are we expecting visitors, Mum?' he called. His mother did not answer immediately, then said, as he heard the waffle-iron sizzle: 'No, what made you think that?'

'You hardly ever make waffles.'

'No one's coming round, dear. No one ever comes here, except those funny birds that you kill.'

A strange feeling possessed the boy, a combination of pain and pleasure, and he squeezed his eyes shut, so tightly that a shower of vivid colours sprang out under the lids.

The Car Wreck

We lived in a small house a stone's throw from the village, my mother and I, and my cousin who was a little older than me.

'We have a good life here, us three women together,' my mother sometimes used to say. I didn't think our life was so good at the time. But it *was*; I can see that now.

The house was grey as stone; it had not even been rendered, and the wires in the concrete still protruded from the walls here and there. My cousin said the house reminded her of a hedgehog, huddling low to the ground on the moor just beyond the banks, with the river meandering past. The banks rose to quite a height in the direction of the river, and there was a small grassy strip on the riverbank itself, where the old wreck of a car lay at the foot of the highest slope. It had been there for many years, since before we came to live in the house. Grass sprouted through the floor and the whole thing had long ago rusted up. I found it ugly seeing rubbish like that littering the beautiful strip of grass, and asked mother how the car had got there and why it hadn't been towed away long ago. She said she thought there had been an accident; the car must have been driven off the bank in the days when the road ran closer to it, before our house was even built, but nothing had been done to remove the wreck; nothing ever got done around here.

My cousin and I used to walk to school in winter, whatever the weather. Every morning we would take the path over the high ground together. The winter I have in mind was when I was ten, and my cousin would turn twelve the following spring. That autumn she had been ill unusually often, so I had to take the path to school on my own. I didn't like that; I often felt lonely on the way and didn't relish walking past the car wreck, whose shape I could make out in the early dawn light at the bottom of the slope. Sometimes it was covered in snow, resembling a creepy igloo with gaping windows and doors.

In mid November the school held a party for all the pupils. The party was to take place at the end of the week, towards evening, so we had to go into the village a second time that day to attend it. Mother helped us to dress up. She had a variety of tricks up her sleeve, but they seemed rather old-fashioned to us, and once we were outside in the winter dusk we pulled off the hair-bands she had forced us to wear. I stuck mine in the pocket of my dress, while my cousin wrapped hers round one of the wires protruding from the concrete wall of the house.

'What do you think Mum will say if she sees it?' I asked.

'I'll pick it up when we come back. She won't go out between now and then,' my cousin said, laughing.

We set off. The weather was still but cold and the snow creaked underfoot on the path. We saw the Northern Lights in the sky, and the mountains, completely white. As we were approaching the bank where the broken car lay, we suddenly heard a peculiar noise. It was like a mumbling, but much louder, and I shivered – not only because my dress was thin.

'Did you hear that?' I asked my cousin. I could see that she was shaken too.

The mumbling sounded again. It increased in volume, carrying clearly from the foot of the bank where the car wreck lay. Extremely frightened by now, I wanted to keep going but my cousin was made of sterner stuff. When she had recovered from her initial fear, she seized my coat sleeve and dragged me with her to the edge of the bank. Looking back,

I saw our tracks in the snow, running side by side from the path.

'Let's keep going,' I said. 'The party will be starting soon.'

'Wait a minute, Hilda,' said cousin Katrín. The mumbling had fallen temporarily silent, but now began again, this time interspersed with growling.

Katrín took my hand and led me down the slope. It was slippery and, losing my footing, I grabbed at her. She steadied me while I got my balance again. We picked our way down to the car wreck which was covered in snow as so often before. Ice crystals glittered faintly on the roof in the pale radiance of the moon and Northern Lights. But I didn't have time to look at glittering crystals. The mumbling and growling grew ever louder, sometimes changing into a violent throat-rattling.

In the driver's seat sat a monster, the like of which I had never seen before. I hope I'll never see anything like it again. Its shape was barely human, yet it had fastened round its body the tatters of the seat belt that still hung beside the seat, or else it had been tied down by someone who had then vanished from the scene; I couldn't tell. This hideous creature jerked and twitched in the seat, rattling and growling incessantly. Suddenly it seemed to catch sight of us and turned a horribly glassy stare in our direction; I saw its eyes clearly in the darkness. I know I screamed. I could hear the wailing as if it came from somewhere else, as if someone else were wailing, and when I looked at my cousin I *saw* that she was screaming too.

We fled up the slope. Clawed our way up, panting and moaning, sliding, the snow whirling up around our skirts. A pitiful growl reached our ears from the car wreck down below. When we finally reached the top, hardly able to catch our breath from exhaustion and terror, we listened for a moment. Now there was complete silence apart from our gasps. But that lasted only an instant before the mumbling began again, and soon it had risen, becoming even louder than before. We raced off, not in the direction of the village but back along the path, home to the stone-grey house. And we held hands as we ran, Katrín and I. When we reached the house I saw her hair-band dangling from one of the wires, pale blue in colour like the river when it flows under ice.

A World Alone

Dedicated to Jens Sigsgaard

i

It was no dream. Some of the buildings had lost their roofs and there were broken window panes everywhere. Doors had fallen off their hinges and all kinds of rubbish lay jumbled in the gardens: battered furnishings, broken garden tools and toys.

He walked along one of the streets in the town, where he had walked long ago in summer when the whole place was alive with people, the houses were freshly painted, all was neat and orderly, and children were playing in the street. A little blonde girl had run into his path with a ball, crying: 'Catch!' She threw the ball to him and, flustered, he had whipped his hands out of his coat pockets and caught it. The ball was blue with white stripes, and when he threw it back to the girl he felt as if he were tossing a tiny planet into the infinity of space. But the girl caught the ball nimbly before he could go any further, smiled at him, then crossed over to the opposite pavement where her three friends were playing hopscotch.

ii

There was nobody there now. Deep, black cracks fissured the tarmac. There were no vehicles to be seen, as if everyone had got into their cars and driven away. The houses stood empty. Most were riddled with cracks like the tarmac; their windows sinister eyeholes in the fading light. He walked on, past the electric substation with its scorched black walls. On the front, beside the heavy door, the following warning could still be deciphered through the soot: 'DANGER/HIGH VOLTAGE'.

He turned up a short side street and from there into the main street, where the old petrol station stood. The tanks were dented and the hoses lay looped and coiled in the slick of oil on the forecourt, like eels in the black mud of a swamp. Something had happened to this town since he was last here in the summer sunshine, the time he threw the ball back to the little girl. There were no cars at the petrol station either. The entrance to the garage shop stood open, the door had gone, and there was no sign of life.

iii

Further up the street stood the library, its windows also gaping and blank, all the glass missing. The light was gradually fading but the streetlights did not come on. Their inner workings had all been smashed, the bulbs too, as if someone had gone systematically from one to the next with a shotgun.

Before long he came across a huge mound, right by the square: books, a vast pile of books, all from the public library, the white labels visible on their spines. They had been brought out here and drenched in petrol, the faint smell of which still tainted the air. Apparently there had been no time to set them alight. He stood for a while before this great heap of literature and read the now barely legible titles on a few of the spines. Towards the bottom of the pile was a dog-eared copy of *Fahrenheit 451* by Ray Bradbury. Perhaps it had been put there deliberately, so the whole thing would burn more easily. Feeling a little chilled, he turned away from this abandoned bonfire and continued on his way.

iv

The church stood on the edge of the square, a whitewashed edifice with a red roof. All the stained glass was broken and its windows were as blank as those of the library and other buildings. One of the doors hung crookedly from the doorframe, the other had vanished. The one that remained had obviously been battered with some heavy instrument, perhaps even a mace. The wood was bashed and dented and great splinters littered the steps, presumably either from the door or the crucifix. Quickening his pace, he made for the further end of the main street. As it narrowed, the buildings grew older and the scene appeared even more desolate.

He was standing by some kind of junk shop when he saw an old woman come out of the house directly opposite. He heard the creaking of a door and all of a sudden there she was in the street, a bowed figure in a dark-blue coat. He started and hurried towards her, but she moved extraordinarily fast for her age, negotiating the fissured tarmac and disappearing into a shadowy alley beyond the junk shop. His footsteps echoed in the alley as he approached. The woman was nowhere to be seen.

'Come out wherever you are!' he called into the alley, but realising he sounded like a policeman, he refrained from repeating it or saying anything else. Instead of entering the alley, he went over to the glassless windows of the junk shop and craned his head into the gloom inside. He glimpsed a table with uneven legs and a broken lamp on the floor beside a heavy armchair. There was a huge vase on a shelf above the table and it struck him as incredible that the vase should still be intact.

'It couldn't be the Holy Grail, could it?' he murmured.

v

The next building along was a photographer's studio. He thought he saw the remnants of a flash lighting up the street when he looked that way. He went over but there was no one there. The glass in the front door had been smashed, like most of the glass in the town. Reaching inside, he undid the lock, turned the door-handle and opened it. The whole studio now resembled one gigantic darkroom. He flicked the switch on the wall but the ceiling light had no bulb. A pungent smell of developing fluid hung in the air, the photos had fallen off the walls onto the floor and there were tinkling fragments of glass everywhere, but he could hardly see the hand in front of his face because the red light that enables one to move around the dark room was absent. He sat down in a chair by the counter, waiting for his fatigue to drain away, and peered out into the street, which was not quite as dark as here inside.

All of a sudden he spotted the old woman again. She crossed the road, now carrying a white plastic bag that appeared almost luminous in the half-light. Rather than returning to the house she had emerged from originally, she continued along the street and up the steps of another, half-ruined building. He watched her without leaving his seat or calling out to her, then snatched up a Polaroid camera from the soot-stained counter. It seemed to have been bashed about. He raised it to his face on an impulse, pointed the lens out of the window and clicked. The apparatus may have been battered but it worked. A blinding flash lit up the darkness and a picture slid out of the back. He peered at it but could see nothing at first. Shoving the photo in the breast pocket of his coat he stood up, went outside and caught sight of the sign: 'PHOTOGRAPHS – FOR EVERY OCCASION,' which had fallen off the wall above the display window. Crouching down, he slowly deciphered the four words in the dusk.

The Writing Room

At the time I had a small room on Holtsgata in the west of Reykjavík, where I was trying to write. I can't quite remember the number of the house, but it might have been 41. That was the winter I was struggling to write a novella which later received the title *Swimming Perch*, but failed to make much of a splash. I was oddly apathetic and dilatory that winter. I got little done, and despite sometimes leaving home in Thingholt at an early hour to go to the room, my efforts at writing generally ended up with my flopping down on the shabby mattress and sleeping for much of the day. By the time I awoke it was growing dark and I didn't feel like staying any longer, so I went home to my wife and child and participated in the housework and parenting.

I didn't in fact have the room to myself because a friend and fellow writer was renting it with me. He later wrote a novel entitled *Herring Days*, so we were both fairly preoccupied with fish, though neither of us had ever gone in for fishing of any kind. During the period in question my roommate was composing poetry, and proved far more diligent at this than I at writing my novella. As a former bank employee, he was used to sitting still and getting something done. Our cohabitation worked well since he was an easy-going type and we never clashed over working hours. If I remember right, there were even occasions when we were both there at the same time, labouring over our contributions to Icelandic literature; I at the desk, he on the mattress using index cards, like Nabokov. On the little table beside the bed an ancient coffee maker boiled and bubbled, producing a strange, black, viscous fluid that we decided by tacit agreement to refer to simply as coffee, although in reality it was something altogether different.

If I happened to be over there very early that autumn, I would sometimes head down to the harbour to breathe in the sea air. Somehow I felt it would invigorate my writing, although perch were of course fresh-water, not sea, fish. But the sea air changed little. I seldom wrote more than a page a day, which I generally threw away the following morning. As a result I took an unusually long time over this little tale, and it did not appear in print until three years after I had left the room for good.

One day I took along a book. This was in November, and I was unusually late leaving home, later than what people with jobs would call second coffee break. The sun would soon be going down. I wanted to get the book bound and had been told about a bookbinder who lived nearby in a back courtyard. But first I went up to the room and turned on the coffee maker. I didn't try to write, just lay down on the mattress and started reading the unbound volume. It was a second edition of *Poems and Stories* by Jóhann Gunnar Sigurdsson, a little work of which I was very fond and wanted to have bound in a hardwearing cover. If I was walking or cycling home to Thingholt from my room, I would frequently stop off at the old churchyard to visit his grave, and that of the old poet Sigurdur Breidfjörd, who made good company for him there.

I nodded off while reading, and must have slept for some time, perhaps more than an hour, because when I awoke, after dreaming about a huge St Bernard that barked at me from behind a saw-toothed white picket fence, the light had faded. The room was filled with the unpleasant odour of coffee that has been stewing too long in the jug over a hot plate, and I turned it off at once, though I hadn't drunk any coffee because I'd dozed off over my book.

I got up, carried the book over to the door and put on my shoes, then turned off the light, closing the door behind me. I wouldn't be back until tomorrow morning at the earliest. I thought it unlikely that my friend would come here this evening to write poetry, since in the evenings he was generally to be found propping up a bar just as diligently as he sat at his writing desk by day.

There was a chilly breeze from the sea when I emerged into the street. After putting on my scarf and the gloves that I kept in the pockets of my anorak, I took the book to the nearby house where I had been told that the bookbinder lived. It was a gloomy little building in a back yard, and when I got there it struck me that the fence in front of the house looked oddly similar to the saw-toothed picket fence of my dream, where the St Bernard had bayed at me, foaming at the mouth, only a short time before.

I knocked at a door which contained four small panes of glass. It was painted green and reminded me somehow of a grassy dell at the height of summer after a gentle shower of rain. No one answered the door, so I knocked again, and at last it opened. The man who appeared in the gap was tall, thin and stooping, with horn-rimmed glasses, hollow cheeks and a strangely claw-like hand that rested on the door handle.

'Good evening,' I said.

'Good evening,' he replied. His voice was hoarse yet almost soft, if it is possible for a voice to be hoarse and soft at the same time. I announced my business and handed him the book. He invited me in, and I entered a front room which was overflowing with shoes in every imaginable state of repair. For a moment I thought I had entered the premises of an old-fashioned cobbler rather than a bookbinder. I could see into a long, badly lit passage with a linoleum floor. A timid-looking woman in a dress darted into a brightly lit kitchen, shutting the door behind her. The bookbinder showed me to the right, into a small room where he had his workshop. Books lay heaped on tables and benches over by windows set low in the whitewashed walls. Some of the books were bound, others half-bound, still others unbound, and some were little more than loose pages strewn all over the place. There were binding tools everywhere, and the air in the workshop was thick with the heavy smell of tobacco smoke. The bookbinder began to fill his pipe – he used Half and Half tobacco – watching me with an enquiring look as he did so.

'You're a literary man?' he asked, sucking in smoke, then puffing it out at me. It put me in mind of one of those spindly cartoon dragons – unhealthy beasts with chronic coughs that intimidate no one yet fondly believe themselves to be alarming enough to scare children.

'I don't know what to say to that,' I answered, letting my eyes stray a little round the room and spotting some binding material in pale red. 'I'd like that sort of binding for the book,' I said. He looked at me almost accusingly, clearly regarding it as a tasteless choice, but took the roll down from the shelf nevertheless and spread it on the table.

'Let's see,' he said, fitting the book to the material, humming quietly all the while. I felt slightly embarrassed at having made it so blatantly obvious that I wasn't a proper literary type, but this did not make me back down over my choice of material. I pretended to be firmly resolved on the matter. I asked for gilding on the spine, and we agreed that he would take in the book for binding and I would pick it up, probably after New Year. I was rather sorry to be parted for so long from Jóhann Gunnar's poetry, but it couldn't be helped.

When we went back into the front room, I heard a strange scratching on the linoleum inside the house. Glancing up, I caught sight of a gigantic St Bernard. It came snuffling along the ill-lit passage to the door of the front room, saliva drooling from its mouth. It did not bark, however, and appeared docile, unlike the dog in my dream. Apart from that it could have been the same animal. I could see no difference – those huge eyes, almost like saucers. I didn't like this; it filled me with a sense of unease. The bookbinder took off his glasses, wiped them on his shirt and put them on again, then reached out to the dog and scratched it behind the ears. The dog moaned and groaned with pleasure, dribbling onto the bookbinder's socks, not that he seemed to notice. Suddenly I saw the woman emerge from what I assumed to be the kitchen, a shaft of light slicing through the passage as she opened the door. Then she closed it behind her, leaving the passage in gloom again, and tiptoed even more timidly than before into another room, affecting not to notice me. I saw that she was wearing an old-fashioned, rose-patterned dress, and the roses – or perhaps they were morning glories – appeared to be black. Perhaps the woman herself was a morning glory, trying to find a foothold in this twilight existence. I thought I could smell raw meat, maybe from the dog; I wasn't sure.

Saying a hasty goodbye, I opened the door and stepped outside. The bookbinder laid his fingers with their long, sharp nails on the door handle as before, still staring at me from behind his glasses; a little more sharply now, I felt.

'Nice fence,' I said in parting, gesturing at the white paling. He slowly closed the door, without answering. I made my way to the gate, lifted the latch and as I did so heard a mournful barking from inside the house. Then the outside light went out and the green door turned black. I hurried for home. It had begun to rain and I wasn't dressed to withstand a soaking, so I started to run, sprinting light-footed along Sólvallagata, then on past the cemetery. This time I did not go in to visit the graves of the two poets. I ran without stopping, hardly tiring. I was filled with elation, a strange, indefinable sense of anticipation. All of a sudden I was a tracker in the Kalahari, with a spear tied to my back, feeling the strap that held it tautening over my chest. I was hunting an eland, a noble antelope. The rainy season had begun and dark clouds rolled overhead.

The Flight to Halmstad

I

They had just started to offer direct flights to the Swedish town of Halmstad. Spotting the advertisement in the paper, I said to my wife: 'You should go, love. You've got an aunt there.'

'You mean you wouldn't be coming?' she asked.

'I'll stay here and try to get something done,' I said.

'But you're on holiday,' she pointed out.

'Exactly,' I said, and carried on reading the paper.

Five days later she was gone. It felt glorious waking up alone that first morning. As I was still on my summer vacation, I did absolutely nothing but sit out on the balcony, reading in the sunshine. I don't know if that counts as getting something done, but it made perfect sense to me.

On the evening of that first day I drank a few beers. Actually, rather more than a few; I got completely pissed and passed out on the sofa just after midnight. By then I must have listened to the same Miles Davis CD a hundred times. It was nearly noon when I surfaced next day. I had been dreaming about a lot of closed doors. In my dream I needed to go to the toilet but couldn't work out the right door, so instead of opening any of them, I urinated into a large ceramic flowerpot. One of the doors suddenly burst open. I have a feeling it was made of rosewood, like kitchen units and coffins in the 1960s. A powerful torch beam was directed at the flowerpot.

It's common knowledge that Dante's description of hell is as nothing compared to the suffering that overtakes one after a heavy bout of beer-drinking. Nevertheless, I dragged myself up later in the day and went outside in the good weather, to make the most of the brilliant sunshine.

I got into the car, though hardly in any fit state to drive, and headed out of town. The car almost steered itself, and before I knew it I had driven all the way out along the Reykjanes peninsula to the lighthouse. I had once known a man who used to be warden there but he was dead now. The house looked derelict; some of its windows were boarded up. A handful of foreign tourists were wandering about down by the sea with their eternal cameras, like pilgrims with amnesia, forever condemned to trying to capture the moment, rather than actually experiencing it. On the way home I drove along the south coast through Grindavík, the Thórkötlustadir area, and from there over the hill to Krýsuvík. The road was a disgrace. I stopped for a while at the little church at Krýsuvík; actually I sat down in one of the pews and remained there for quite some time with bowed head, still feeling rough. On the road past Lake Kleifarvatn I came within a millimetre of death, when a large jeep hurtled round a rocky spur and brushed past my car with a crazy honking. The incident left me trembling all over, and I continued at a snail's pace, taking an eternity to reach town.

That evening I was feeling sufficiently recovered to have another beer. I relaxed on the sofa in front of the television, sipping my beer, and giving Miles Davis a complete rest. The phone rang. It was my wife. She told me what a fantastic time she was having in Halmstad; her aunt had the whole house to herself since her husband died.

'Nice for her,' I muttered into the phone. We spoke briefly. I hung up and carried on watching a Jack Nicholson film, taking swigs from the can from time to time. After the film the radio news came on, signalling the end of the day's broadcast, and the announcer read in neutral tones:

'Yesterday John Roebuck, one of the world's top cyclists, died when a wasp flew into his mouth on the eleventh day of the Tour de France, causing his throat to swell up and suffocate him. He was in fourth place in the race at the time.'

I turned off the television and stared out of the window for a while, feeling the cool beer sliding down my throat.

II

The days were monotonous. The weather was almost invariably warm with brilliant sunshine. Then abruptly my summer holiday was over. Yet I was still alone. I went back to work, driving over to Kópavogur every morning. My wife rang occasionally. She said she'd be coming home soon. I was a bit fed up with being alone. It had been liberating for the first few days – a bit like the way people describe a visit to a nudist colony. But after that the novelty wears off, and everyone is glad to put their clothes back on.

August passed, to be succeeded by September. I was still alone. Neither my wife nor I are mobile-phone types, so I didn't hear from her very often, though she did make contact at regular intervals from her aunt's home phone. Yet whenever I wanted to ring that number to hear how she was, it was engaged. I was starting to get suspicious.

'Are you sure you're at your aunt's?' I asked her once when she called. There was an uncomfortable silence over the phone, then she hung up. I tried to call her straight back, but the line was engaged as usual.

October appeared on the calendar with its pictures of dogs. Its passing was slow and tedious, alternating between wind and rain, and I was tired of cooking for one. I couldn't be bothered to tidy up and the flat had become a bit of a dump, typical of a modern recluse; beer cans and dirty socks everywhere. Absolutely nothing happened.

III

November arrived, also packed with dismal weather. One day, thinking that things couldn't go on like this, I decided to book a flight to Halmstad. But now I was told it wasn't possible; they'd had to drop that route late in the summer due to lack of demand. Of course, I could fly to Copenhagen or Gothenburg, and from there to Halmstad, but a kind of apathy had taken hold of me and I never got round to booking a ticket. I regretted ever having the bright idea of sending her to her aunt's. The word 'aunt' developed sinister connotations in my mind.

IV

It's December now, the run-up to Christmas has begun. I'm not sleeping well. It's strange, but I generally sleep better in the light summer nights than in the long, dark winter ones. When darkness falls, I start brooding over stupid old mistakes, tossing and turning, grinding my teeth and mumbling 'idiot' over and again to myself.

I never hear from my wife. Now when I ring the aunt's number, a dreary, unfamiliar voice says something in Swedish, which I take to mean simply: '*This number is not connected.*' I'm going to spend Christmas out west in Stykkishólmur with Mum. She's invited me so often. Apart from that, I suppose I'll always be alone.

Morning in the West of Town

The sun was shining on the surrounding roofs when he came out of the house. He walked down the beaten-earth path to the sea, which lay smooth as a mirror right across the bay; Mount Akrafjall shimmering in the morning light, Skardsheidi wreathed in pale-blue mist beyond: an ideal subject for a watercolour. He picked his way down the shingle bank with the help of his stick and stood for a while at the tidemark, gazing out to sea, then lowered his eyes to the ground at his feet and began to examine the life of the shore. There was a starfish, a small crab, and a sand-hopper writhing in the sand. He prodded the starfish with his stick, then picked it up along with the crab and put them in his coat pocket. After that he slowly retraced his steps up the shingle bank and along the narrow path between the turf-roofed crofts, to the wooden house where he lived.

Opening the door, he went inside, took off his galoshes and shoes, and hung his coat on a peg, having first removed the crab and starfish from his pocket. He carried them carefully up the steep wooden staircase. Upstairs was the study, where all his books were kept; innumerable books, the majority bound in brown leather and arranged according to size. Hanging on the walls between the bookshelves were pictures of dead poets; Goethe was there, and Schiller beside him. They provided him with company, while never distracting him. The desk over by the window held a pile of paper, pen handles, inkstands, dictionaries and other reference works. A sunbeam fell through the glass onto the desk, tempting him to sit down to work. He went over and laid the crab and starfish on the corner of the desk beside a thick dictionary.

He took his seat at the desk. Ever since the sun had shone more brightly that spring, he had found it easier to settle down to write or draw. But the winter had been hard. He had often woken with a gnawing sense of dread in the middle of the night, unable to get back to sleep. He didn't know what he dreaded. He did not regard death with terror. And if that was so, what else could there be to dread?

He picked up a large-format reference book and began to turn the pages. It was a book about marine animals, illustrated with black-and-white diagrams. The text was in Danish and he read for a while, then returning it to its place, he took a pencil and started to draw on a sheet of paper, glancing every now and then at the crab. Little by little he reproduced the sea creature on paper, complete with serrated claws.

He was hedged about by dark books, bound in the hides of land animals. The poets in the portraits looked somehow expressionless and rigid, as if forever frozen in a state of lyrical exaltation. Their eyes stared blankly at his back as he sat drawing at the desk, with a flowerpot beside him on the windowsill. He bent over the desktop, oblivious to everything but the crab that he had found in the black sand down on the shore, site of his daily pilgrimage to inspect the sea's offerings.

He stopped drawing, pushed the piece of paper aside and picked up an exercise book, marked *B.G.* in ornamental lettering on the front. He began to write furiously, dipping his pen from time to time in the inkwell. It was a long letter. He didn't know who he was writing to, but suspected it was himself.

★

After a while he pushed his chair back from the desk, went over to the bookcase and searched briefly on the shelves before pulling out a book. It was the second volume of Goethe's *Poems* in the original German. He turned to page 296 and muttered the poem to himself, before closing the book and returning to his desk, where he sat down and continued his writing.

The flower on the windowsill was red; its acid-green leaves, translucent in the sunshine, looked just like ears listening for notes from on high.

The Bird Painter from Boston

I was here to paint birds. I landed at Keflavík airport early in the morning and took the airport bus with all my bags to Reykjavík. The weather was fine, but the lava plains were a dispiriting, lifeless grey, and I saw no birds. This struck me as odd, but it was not until we reached Hafnarfjördur that I saw seabirds swarming over the shore.

The apartment I had taken was on Birkimelur, not far from this old graveyard. It was a clean, bright apartment in a block, which I had rented at a reasonable rate through an Icelandic ornithologist friend of mine, who had encouraged me to come over. I had already painted birds in Mexico and Patagonia, and written accounts of my trips. The plan was to write a similar account of my stay here.

It was near the end of June. Reykjavík made a pleasant impression on me; a neat little town, with a bracing air. I had procured myself a street map, and straight after lunch set out for a walk to see the city. I lingered for quite some time in the old cemetery, which was most unexpected. Thrushes and redpolls sang in the gnarled branches, and you'd have had to have been a corpse not to have been moved by their music.

In the evening I went downtown and walked into a rather shady bar. No one spoke to me and I didn't like the atmosphere; it reminded me of the kind of rough joints I've visited in Chicago. There wasn't a breath of wind as I walked across the bridge over the lake on my way home, and here I found birdlife. I spent a long time watching the Arctic terns cleaving the air with their tails, snipping it with their scissor-like wings, and screeching. I had given up the idea of travelling to broaden my mind and make me wiser. Some people believe travelling makes them more intelligent. But I've met people who have visited every corner of the world and are so dumb that it is inconceivable they were any dumber before they set out. The Arctic tern flies here all the way from Antarctica, then flies right back. It has a good sense of direction, I'll give it that, but otherwise I don't think its intelligence is in any proportion to the vast journeys it undertakes.

I came home to the apartment. The evening light was so attractive in the living room that I sat down at the oak table by the window and took out my drawing paper and colours. I drew the terns in flight, from memory. That's not how I work as a rule. I usually have an example of the bird in front of me when I draw, but this evening (maybe it was the alcohol) I wanted to draw birds from memory. Dissatisfied with the outcome, however, I scrunched up the pages and threw them in the bin.

Next day I went to see my ornithologist friend. He had studied at the university at home in Boston, and was pretty good in his field. He took me to a car rental place where I hired a Land Rover for an exorbitant price. Just as well my finances were in good shape. I drove hesitantly through the fast-moving, chaotic traffic back to Birkimelur. There I spent another night, but the following day I was planning to take a day trip to Snæfellsnes.

There was a light drizzle when I awoke next morning. I loaded my stuff into the car: telescopes and cameras, sketch books and rain gear, as well as the small rifle I had borrowed, and drove at a sedate pace out of town. There wasn't much traffic as yet. I saw on the map that the mountain in front of me was called *Esja*; a long, imposing bulk, half-obscured by cloud. I drove along its foot for a considerable time until I reached the tunnel. I've never liked tunnels. I don't know whether it's because they touch the primitive man in me, conjuring up dim memories of fires licking over cave walls and animal pictures painted in blood on the pitch-black rock. Or whether it's because you are back in the womb, as the psychologists say, and it's actually a shock to emerge into the daylight again – like a second birth. Who knows, but for me, far from being a shock, it was a great relief to re-emerge into the open air, even though the sky was overcast. I dreaded having to pass through the tunnel again on my way back. Maybe I would take the road around Hvalfjördur instead, although I saw from the map that it was inordinately long. Were they still whaling in this 'Whale Fjord'? Not that it mattered to me. I was at odds with most of my fellow Americans on the subject, for it seemed to me a far worse thing to massacre people in far-flung parts of the world, the way my country did in the name of freedom and humanity.

The countryside was teeming with wading birds on either side of the road through the *Mýrar* or 'Marshes', north of a picturesque little village called Borgarnes. More than once I had a redshank nearly fly into my windshield. I turned on the wipers, since it had started to rain, and the comfortable but insistent swishing noise reminded me of that day in Patagonia, the only day it rained. The one day in six months that a drop of rain fell from the sky. I had been driving a Land Rover then as well, along a road even bleaker than this one.

I had just passed a sign saying 'ELDBORG', without taking the turning, when I saw a hitchhiker stick out his thumb on the roadside. He was wearing orange waterproofs, and looked wet and cold. I stopped and picked him up. He turned out to be French, a professor of linguistics at the University of Marseille. In spite of his job title, his English was none too good. But we could maintain a conversation of sorts about what we saw along the way, which wasn't much in the rain. Soon wearying of the driving and the fitful conversation, I yawned surreptitiously. I think he noticed. At any rate, he suddenly clammed up. Some time later I asked him where he was going and he answered that he was heading for Arnarstapi, and pointed it out on the map he was holding. I decided to go with the flow and abandon my plan to return to Reykjavík that evening.

As I took the turning down to the village, two ravens flew in front of the car. Preoccupied with studying their flight, the way they used their wings, I hit some loose gravel and near as damn it drove off the road. I saw out of the corner of my eye that the Frenchman was petrified, but he put a good face on it and didn't even say *merde*.

The guesthouse in this curious little fishing village was white with a red roof, which appears to be the most popular colour combination for houses in this country. There was a white wooden board by the broken-down gate, with 'GUESTHOUSE' painted in clumsy black letters. They had precisely two vacancies, though in reality I have a feeling these were the only guestrooms in the house. The Frenchman went to his room without even thanking me for the lift. I shrugged and entered my cubbyhole. It wasn't so bad. The window faced northwest by my reckoning, which is where that famous Snæfellsjökull glacier was supposed to be, although it was currently invisible. There was a television in the room and I watched a British soap. Afterwards I decided to go out, taking the binoculars and camera with me. First I walked down to the bizarre harbour, where kittiwakes glided ceaselessly along the low cliffs and out over the dazzling white boats. The scene reminded me somehow of certain little fishing villages in Italy. I don't know quite what it was, but there was something about it. The sea was extraordinarily green and aggressive here; nowhere have I had a better sense of what Melville says about Noah's flood being not yet over since two-thirds of the planet are still under water.

A small path climbed up from the harbour to the edge of the cliff, then continued along the precipice. For an instant, my thoughts swung to Jessica, but I pushed them away again. Birds circled overhead, all kinds of seabirds. I tried to remember some of their Latin names, but these have never really been my forte. I find them a little dumb: as if birds could care less what they are called in a dead language. But that's just my particular quirk, a limitation that I don't advertise to my colleagues in the ornithological world.

I came to a gigantic opening in the rock, a yawning abyss down to the sea many metres below. It emitted a menacing sucking and booming, reminding me of the tunnel I had driven through that morning. I felt overcome all of a sudden. A great black-backed gull shot up through the rock opening with an ominous beating of its wings. Its cold wingtip seemed almost to stroke against my face, as if it were a brush and wanted to paint me black, paint my cheek like one of those Sioux warriors on their way to do battle against the *wasichus* who stole their land in the Black Hills. I suddenly remembered what my grandmother used to say when I stayed with her in Lexington as a little boy: 'It's no good flying on stork's wings.'

I got to my feet, shuddering with the cold, and walked back to the guesthouse. There I asked to use the phone in the lobby and called home. I called Jessica. She didn't answer immediately. But just as I was about to hang up, she picked up the phone.

'Yes?' she said. I sensed her voice flowing down the line, over that vast distance, and tingled all over with warmth.

'Jessica,' I said. 'Darling Jess, I'm coming home. I've quit painting birds.' I hung up without ever hearing her answer. The woman in reception, kindly and middle-aged, looked at me bewildered.

'I'm going home,' I said to her in English. 'I'm going to quit writing books, quit everything I've been doing up till now.'

She nodded, still looking rather bewildered, then smiled and said: 'Yes.'

The Lost Grimms' Fairytale

My wife went ahead through the trees. We had been walking for over two hours in the forestry plantation, following any number of enchanting, shady paths and stopping in a little clearing to drink coffee from a thermos flask. It had been a good walk; we had talked more in those two hours than we usually did in two days.

'Look at the wood cranesbill over there,' she said, pointing to some tree roots close to the path. I went up to her and peered at where she was pointing.

'Pretty,' I said.

'Divine,' she said. 'I'd like to pick a bunch.'

'I don't think you're allowed to here,' I said.

We walked on, and now she took my hand and we strolled hand in hand in the sunshine, something we had not done for a long time.

The lovely path rounded a bend. The pines looked as if they had been cut out of a painting by Cézanne. I inhaled deeply and felt a sense of well-being flowing through my body. Then we spied some people stooping in the shadows among the trees.

'Oh look, they're picking mushrooms,' my wife cried in delight.

'Yes, I think are,' I agreed, picturing those quaint wicker baskets, familiar from French pastoral paintings, filled with mushrooms. 'Some mushrooms are really poisonous, though. They could be your last supper.'

'But they're not like that here?' she asked.

'I'm not so sure,' I replied.

At that moment two dogs came bounding out of the trees, past the stooping figures. We stiffened up and let go of each other's hands. They were enormous beasts; one a Doberman, the other an Alsatian. They raced towards us, eerily silent and menacing. The Alsatian reached us first. It snapped at my wife's coat. She screamed and flung herself behind me for protection. The Doberman paused, staring into my eyes for a second. Then it attacked without warning, in dead silence, biting me on the thigh. I was more stunned than afraid. I hadn't for a moment dreamed that it would actually attack.

I remember looking up at the sky, just after it had bitten me, and thinking it was as if the blueness had frozen in the midst of the summer warmth. It looked so cold all of a sudden. This is what it's like to be bitten by a snake, I thought. My eyes returned to the dog. The owners had straightened up, holding their baskets, which *were* made of wicker, just as I had imagined. They called off the dogs, in what seemed a ludicrously doting tone of voice, and the brutes obeyed reluctantly, the Alsatian giving us a low growl. It was all still so surreal, as if time had stood still and was never going to jerk into motion again. Like a power station in a deep canyon, brought to a halt by the iron clutch of winter and locked in silence until spring.

'Did he bite you?' the man asked, slipping a lead onto the Doberman. His voice was anxious. He knew I could easily have the brute put down.

'How can you ask that, for Christ's sake?' I snarled through pursed lips. The pain had begun to make itself felt, and with that, time seemed to have limped into motion again. My wife still seemed paralysed, cowering behind me in a dejected huddle, but now suddenly stepped out in front and yelled at the woman who was putting a lead on the Alsatian:

'What were you thinking of?'

She didn't usually raise her voice, except perhaps to me. I found it strange hearing her shout like that at a complete stranger.

'I don't know,' the woman admitted, standing with the lead in her hand. The dogs' eyes were fixed on us. My brain was still partially numb. I didn't have the presence of mind to do anything but limp back to our car, which we had left at the car park several hundred metres away. I felt the wound catch with every step. The empty thermos flask rattled against the cups in my backpack.

'You should be more careful,' my wife hissed at the couple, who stood with bowed heads under the pines, holding their baskets of mushrooms and their dogs.

'It's totally against the law!' I yelled over my shoulder, on my painful progress to the car. When we got in, I noticed that blood had begun to seep through my torn trousers.

'You'll have to get a Tetanus jab,' my wife said.

'Do you think so?' I asked.

'No question,' she replied.

'There's no paradise without a serpent,' I said, shifting the passenger seat as far back as it would go, and stretching out my leg to try to relax the thigh muscles and alleviate the pain. My wife started the car and drove out of the gravel car park. The road was very dry; a veil of dust hung over the neighbouring trees. There was still not a cloud in the sky.

'Did you see that dog's eyes?' I said.

'Which one?'

'The one that bit me.'

'No, the other one was bad enough.' She accelerated, and we drove past the lake. Someone was out fishing in a boat. I hoped the fish would have the sense to avoid the vicious hooks. I hoped the mushrooms were poisonous.

Winter Hotel

I had been four nights now at Hotel Hvanneyri in the sub-arctic town of Siglufjördur. It was mid January and snow had fallen ceaselessly throughout the North Iceland Chess Tournament. The last round was due to take place tomorrow – we were playing according to the Monrad system. I was in the junior league, and had got on reasonably well, despite needlessly throwing away two games. I had a tendency to abandon positions which, on closer inspection, turned out not to have been so hopeless after all.

It was snowing when I went out for a walk towards evening. I was feeling homesick and lonely; disappointed at not having come top in my class. The town seemed overwhelmingly depressing in this weather. There were high drifts at the corner of every building and the roads were almost impassable to cars. Few people were out and about. Old factory buildings with ugly chimneys lent the scene an even drearier air.

I never want to come here again, I thought to myself, as I made my way down to one of the jetties in the winter dusk. I stood there as the snow fell thickly in the stillness, staring out at the pitch-black sea for a while, then turned, tucking my head into my shoulders, and trudged back to the hotel. It was completely dark by the time I reached it. I went up to my room and lay down, but the walls were thin and someone was playing irritating music in the room next door. It was a creepy hotel, everyone said it was haunted, but I hadn't been aware of anything during the four nights I'd been there. My sleep had been fitful though; I kept starting awake and looking out of the window, only to see the perpetual snowflakes falling.

The music stopped. I nodded off and slept for about two hours; when I awoke it was time for supper. I went downstairs to the dining room, where the matches were held during the day. The rounds began after lunch. I had finished my games unusually early that day, after drawing twice in quick succession. In the second game I played black, used the Sicilian defence and was lucky to get off with a draw. My opponent was not in a mood for battle, however, and accepted the draw unthinkingly.

There were few people in the dining room. But the food was quite reasonable. I sat down by a window and looked out as I ate. Then two contestants from the adult league staggered in; both were ranked high in the tournament and in with a chance of a prize but were now considerably the worse for wear, in spite of the final round tomorrow. They seated themselves at a table at the far end of the room, where they proceeded to conduct a noisy conversation. Closing my ears, I finished my meal, draining the last drop from my bottle of Coke, and stood up. One of the boys from the junior league had invited me for a drink in his room the night before, having persuaded someone to buy alcohol for him at the liquor store, but I had declined; I hadn't got the hang of drinking. He said I was a wimp. I didn't care.

I went into the TV lounge and watched a couple of programmes. The reception was poor and every now and then a blizzard appeared on screen to emulate the one outside. At half-past ten I got to my feet and went up to my room on the floor above. When I came upstairs there was a commotion on the landing: it was the chess players from earlier, now even drunker. I slipped past them without their apparently noticing.

The landing light went out as soon as they disappeared

downstairs, and I was on my own. The high window in the end wall admitted a faint light. I saw the snow coming down heavily outside and it occurred to me that if the roads were blocked, I might not be able to get home after the final game tomorrow. The thought filled me with dismay; I didn't want to stay here a moment longer.

When I opened the door to my room, the lock gave a strange click as if something had broken. I extracted the key with difficulty but it turned out to be intact. I put it in my pocket and closed the door behind me. The room was plainly furnished: a bed with a spring mattress and wrought-iron bedstead, a shabby armchair, a basin and mirror, a wardrobe, and a reddish-coloured carpet on the floor. The shower was out on the landing. I usually made a dash for it in my dressing gown, feeling almost like a patient in hospital. As a matter of fact, there was something 'sickly' about this hotel. Perhaps it had been a hospital before; I didn't know. Feeling a sudden urge to take a shower before bed, I put on my dressing gown and went out. The landing was still in darkness and no one was about, but I could hear a hubbub of raised voices downstairs that I couldn't quite account for; maybe it was the television.

When I emerged from the shower onto the landing, my eyes were drawn once more to the high window at the end of the corridor. The snow had stopped at last. There was even a small star twinkling in the sky over the roof of the building opposite. It was a cheering sight. It increased my chances of getting home soon and escaping this gloomy building where everyone was aloof from me, everyone my adversary.

I experienced the same problem with the lock as before, only this time it was even harder to turn the key and open the door, but I succeeded in the end and it didn't matter anyway since I was going home tomorrow. My mind held an echo of rejoicing at the thought. The star over the rooftop must have been my lucky star. But the moment I entered my room I knew I was not alone. I was conscious of some indefinable, alien presence. A cold shudder ran down my spine, although I was still warm from my shower.

Why does this have to happen now? I thought. The curtain was drawn. It was quite dark in the room, and I could see little but the faint light from outside, blocked by the thick curtain. I noticed for the first time how ugly its pattern was, with the glow from the streetlight behind it highlighting the coarse weave of the gigantic, almost malevolent roses, machine-stitched onto the cheap material.

I sensed that this *presence* emanated from the wardrobe which was very tall and deep. It wasn't so much that it was evil, more that it was filled with loneliness and a sense of impending death, and utterly out of place here in this room with me, in the darkness. I walked hesitantly over to the reading lamp by the bed and switched it on. The bright glare flooded every nook and cranny, yet now its light seemed somehow cheerless. Dispiriting. I went over to the wardrobe and opened it. All it contained was my suitcase and two chess books that I had brought along: *Bobby Fischer: My 60 Memorable Games* and *Tal's 100 Best Games*. I remembered that Mikhail Tal, 'the Magician from Riga', once said: 'You must take your opponent into a deep dark forest where 2+2=5, and the path leading out is only wide enough for one.'

I left the light on when I went to bed. Although I didn't like the glare it emitted, it was better than nothing. The music had started up again in the room next door, but this time the noise was welcome. I felt an urge to call out and ask whoever it was to turn the volume even higher, then realised that it was the drunk chess players, who now began to shout in competition with the music.

Somehow, in spite of everything, I managed to get to sleep and did not wake until late in the morning. I had dream after dream, all of them nightmarish, filled with some mysterious malevolence that penetrated my sleep, like smoke from an oil lamp. I woke up just in time for the final round, lost my game, and ended up in sixth place. The two men, who were competing in the master's league and sang themselves hoarse to the music in the room next door to mine last night, failed to show up for their final games.

The snow started falling again around the time I set off home in the car with my uncle who had come to fetch me. He drove in silence, with chains on all the wheels and the wipers working away constantly, while I sat beside him in the darkness, dwelling on my experience the night before in that horrible old hotel. It was such an indescribable relief to get away that it didn't matter if my uncle hardly addressed a word to me. Even my performance in the tournament no longer mattered.

★

I didn't visit Siglufjördur again for twenty-five years, by which time I had long ago given up chess. This was last summer, in a 23°C heat-wave. The town was enveloped in a sultry haze. The tumbledown docks had been demolished; a renovated Hotel Hvanneyri was enjoying a new lease of life. I approached over the Siglufjördur pass and began my visit with a walk in the pleasant forestry plantation inland from the town, where I sat down on a bench in a shady clearing and thought idly about those long-ago winter days, wondering if this could really be the same place, if I was the same person as then. Although I no longer played chess, I still had a tendency to give up on things in life before it was certain that all was lost. Then I began to wonder what could have been in my room that January night before my departure. Could it have been anything other than my imagination? Here on the bench, in the muggy heat among the trees, it was hard to believe in any malignant forces lurking in the dark corners of existence – in an old hotel, of all places. I continued to brood on the question, without coming to any conclusion. Lying beside the bench was a branch that had been lopped off at the trunk. I picked it up and, before I knew it, was calculating how many chessmen could be carved from its wood.

The Carpentry Workshop

I often spent time with Dad in his workshop, watching him make things for our neighbours and others, and helping out as much as I could, though I was only nine years old that summer. The workshop was small and dark, yet it often seemed more fun in there with Dad and his brother than playing outside in the narrow street with the other boys. Jakob hardly ever wanted to be inside making things. He used to laugh at me, calling me a Daddy's boy. I retorted that he was a Mummy's boy. At that he became rather sheepish and stopped teasing me. I felt almost sorry for him, knowing that I had found out his weak spot. It was very obvious to me that Mum had some kind of power over him, but I couldn't understand it. She didn't have that kind of power over me, though of course I loved her. Jakob and I had never got on particularly well, despite being brothers and sleeping side by side in a little cubbyhole with a window high up under the ceiling. The boys he played with wanted nothing to do with me.

'Go and play with your hammer,' they sneered. 'Careful you don't hit your fingers.'

I couldn't care less if they didn't want to play with me. I just went back into the workshop, and Dad's brother Aron said:

'You'll make a carpenter if you go on like this, my lad.'

I liked the sound of that, and picking up a saw, laboured away in the corner, cutting a big piece of wood in two. Next, I planed the two halves. They were slightly different lengths.

Dad looked at me and asked:

'What are you going to make out of those?'

And I answered: 'A kite maybe; they can fly really high.'

But I never did make anything with those pieces of wood. Later that summer something happened that put me off carpentry forever.

★

Nóra, my younger sister, fell down the well in the road. The well was nearly empty and her skull cracked in the fall. Uncle Aron carried her home, and he and Dad made a coffin for her. I sat in the corner of the workshop, watching this melancholy task. It was early in the morning the day after the accident, not yet light outside, and a single lamp burned on the planing bench. As they bent over the newly planed boards, I listened to the hammering; it sounded as if it came from the bowels of the earth. None of us said a word; the lantern guttered on the bench. It was then that I decided I would never do any woodwork again. I kept to my word. Later, when things were almost back to normal, Dad said that I should have carried on and joined him in the carpentry business. I answered that two carpenters in the family were enough, and that I would take up woodwork again if he could build a staircase to heaven. He said he couldn't do that. I said in that case I would weave one out of words. He shot me a glance when I said this. We were standing outside the workshop late in the afternoon, the sun was low in the sky and Dad's face was lit up by a glow from beyond the rooftops. He was brandishing a hand drill, as if he meant to drill a hole in the sky as soon as darkness fell, so the light could shine through from behind. For that is what the stars are: holes in the night sky through which the light streams. The sky looked so close that it seemed as if Dad need only take his hand drill and climb the steps up the outside wall onto the flat roof of the house.

★

Now, in that same light, I can feel the nails in my palms. Two strips of different lengths, like the time I was going to make the kite. While waiting for darkness to fall, I remember what it was like in Dad's workshop: handling the tools, watching Aron sawing out a pattern while laughing at some comment of Dad's. Sitting on a heap of wood shavings one evening, staring at the flame of the lantern on the windowsill. You could hear people passing by in the dusk, grown-ups and children. Someone was crying, then nothing more was heard. I remember the whole thing better with my eyes closed. Everything is better with one's eyes closed; even the sun seems brighter that way. Now I can finish weaving this staircase from words, with eyes closed, like a blind man weaving a basket for bread.

Watershed

They had been in the Faroe Islands for five days when they went to visit Saksun. It was raining as they drove out of Tórshavn, just as it had rained every day since they arrived. They found it strange driving around a country where the distances between villages were so short that even the longest journeys were little further than the quick hop over the mountains from Reykjavík to Selfoss at home.

It was past midday when their car pulled up beside the houses of Saksun. The sky was overcast but no rain was falling here and the mountains were free from fog. Saksun is an extraordinary, romantic place. It would have been the perfect setting if Keats, Shelley and Byron had ever needed a retirement home.

'It's beautiful here,' the woman said as the car stopped.

'Almost too beautiful,' he said, undoing his seat belt. He looked round at his son in the back seat. 'Are you coming out to have a look round or are you going to mope in the car as usual?' He couldn't quite hide the irritation in his voice.

'Car,' came the monosyllabic reply. The boy glanced out of the window at the black houses with their turf roofs and the white church standing a little below them.

'Won't you come with us, Jonni?' the woman asked.

'Leave him be,' the man said. 'It's hopeless,' he added with emphasis. Opening the door, he got out and stretched, then went round and took a green backpack out of the boot.

'What do you need the pack for?' asked the woman.

'I'm going to take a stroll down to the sea and out along the bay.'

'And what am I supposed to do in the meantime?'

'You could look round the church and museum.'

The woman stared at him. She seemed hardly able to believe he was in earnest. Then she looked wearily down at the sea and said: 'Right.'

It was the middle of July and the place was crowded with tourists, drawn as always by the charm of the setting. The man put on his waterproof, a standard precaution here in the islands, like fastening your seat belt. He set off and the woman watched him walk down to the sea. All of a sudden she felt like a fisherman's wife, seeing her husband off to his ship. But there was no ship in the cove, and a gloomy stillness hung over the scene. The mountains enclosing it on every side were a deep shade of green, a colour found nowhere else on earth.

He adjusted the backpack, and by the time he had climbed down to the beach his whole being felt lighter. Taking a quick glance back, he saw her walk over to the church in her yellow raincoat. He waved but she didn't wave back. Perhaps she wasn't looking his way. Reaching into the zip-up compartment on the front of his pack, he fished out a small pair of binoculars and directed them at the car. The boy was still sitting in the back seat, absorbed in his comics as usual.

The man walked on, reached the foot of the mountain and began to pick his way along the beach that lay at the bottom of the steep slope, interspersed with the occasional rocky outcrop. At one point he had to scramble a bit in order to reach the end of the promontory at the mouth of the cove. He managed to negotiate this difficult section with ease, experiencing none of his usual vertigo. It was as if he were a different person. Or perhaps it was only now, after all these years, that he was himself. He looked back from his vantage point at the end of the promontory. He had been walking at a leisurely pace, stopping to examine pebbles or watch birds, so it must be more than an hour since he set out.

Picking up the binoculars again, he scanned the area round the church. A trickle of tourists came into view in their multicoloured waterproofs, as if a rainbow had crash-landed in the field, scattering it with fragments. Next he looked over at the little huddle of black houses, but saw no one he knew. Then he looked up at the car, or rather at where the car had been. It had gone. There was nothing there now but a tight knot of coaches. After staring hard through the binoculars for a while, he lowered them and said quietly: 'All right then.'

He climbed up to the highest point of the promontory where the Atlantic Ocean rose into view. There he sat down and took a sandwich and a can of Føroya Malt from his backpack. He felt soothed by the booming of the sea. Somehow it reminded him of the humming of the hot-water pipes in the walls at home, when he used to lie in the darkness as a little boy, unable to sleep, listening to the sound behind the wooden panelling and feeling safe from all the ills of the world. It dawned on him that it must have been like that in the womb, a constant booming in one's ears.

He sat there for a long time. When he stood up again, instead of heading back the same way, he threaded along the narrow knife-edge of the ridge. He didn't suffer in the slightest from the vertigo that had dogged him like a shadow all these years.

Berry Juice

I

The first thing I spotted were the bends of the river as we came east over the hill in the twilight and the plains spread out before us. Next, the cluster of houses came into view, with lights on in the odd window. We drove up to one of the outermost buildings, a whitewashed, two-storey house with a sizeable garden of trees around it, in some places obscuring the windows.

'You've got the key?' I asked Gudbjörn. He fished in his jacket pocket and handed it over, as I turned off the main road towards the house. The gate was shut, and Gudbjörn got out to open it. He cut a peculiarly ungainly figure in the beam of the headlights, reminding me of a funeral director as he opened the gate with slow, deliberate movements.

Instead of getting back in the car, he walked on up to the lightless house. I parked in the yard and got out. The air was damp and redolent with the scent of the trees.

'A good place to stay,' I said, walking up the steps. Gudbjörn went over to one of the trees below the house and relieved himself. 'Ah, it's good to take a leak,' he said. I pretended not to hear him. The journey had taken longer than expected and I'd begun to find him tiresome.

I opened the door. A faint odour of damp and linseed oil met us from the hallway. I turned on the light and we stepped inside, closing the door behind us.

'Did you lock the car?' asked Gudbjörn.

'Of course I did,' I said. 'You don't leave a car full of books unlocked. Not even in a country village.'

'Does anyone want to steal books these days?' he asked. 'It's not like many people even want to buy…'

Without bothering to reply, I made straight for the kitchen with the plastic bag containing food for breakfast and instant coffee powder. I put the milk in the fridge. There was a slight smell of mould inside and the light-bulb in the cooler compartment blinked continually at erratic intervals, as if sending me an important message in Morse code that I couldn't understand.

'Which room do you want?' Gudbjörn asked when I returned to the hall. All at once his expression seemed almost submissive, as if it had finally dawned on him who was in charge on this trip.

'Are there only two?'

'Yes.'

'I really don't mind,' I said.

'Then I'd like to sleep here,' he said, pointing to the larger room. It had curious wallpaper, featuring a rather depressing faded ivy design. Above the bed hung a garish, almost glow-in-the-dark, painting of the Saviour with '*Come unto me*' written in flowery script at the bottom.

'You'll be nice and snug in there,' I said, carrying my little case into the other room, which had no wallpaper, only rather cracked, yellow paint. No picture of Jesus either, but a bookshelf by the head of the bed. Perhaps the books had been sold to the people who lived here by salesmen like us. There was a floral cover on the bed but no curtain at the window, where branches fumbled greenly against the glass. All I knew about the people who had formerly lived here was that the man had been a carpenter and bookbinder, and the woman had kept hens in a little coop above the house. It would take too long to explain how we came to be staying here, though it was rather an odd story.

II

Not wanting to go to bed straight away, I went into the sitting room where Gudbjörn was standing in the darkness, looking out of the window. Joining him, I glimpsed the shape of a dark shed between the tree trunks; probably the hen-house.

'There's no TV,' Gudbjörn said.

'You could read.'

'You know reading bores me.'

'Spoken like a true bookseller,' I said, my mood improving.

I suggested checking out what the cellar had to offer. We opened the door and descended the gloomy stairs to be met by a powerful stench of mould.

It had once housed a very small carpentry and bookbinding workshop. The place was cluttered with bookbinding materials, tools, planes, chisels and different kinds of saws. It looked as if the carpenter had walked out in the middle of a job. The light I switched on was dim, a single bulb that can't have been more than 25 watts. The books he had been binding when he departed (into the next world, of course) were for the most part antiquated religious tracts, some in Gothic script. Yet among them were several works of erotica illustrated with rather risqué black-and-white photos. Gudbjörn picked up one of these and turned its pages with interest.

'Look at that,' he said with a leer, showing me one of the pictures. 'That's what centrefolds used to be like in the old days.' The old man had clearly completed his binding of this book. It was a very tasteful piece of work, with neat gilt lettering on the spine spelling out 'FRENCH EROTICA'.

'Not bad at all,' I remarked.

'Bags I take this one,' Gudbjörn said.

I wanted to object but stopped myself, merely muttering:

'Since you can't be bothered to read,' and turned to a shelf on the wall containing several grimy, dust-covered bottles with handwritten labels. They seemed for the most part to contain glue or thinner, but there was one bottle marked *Berry Juice*. I wondered if the carpenter kept alcohol in the bottle and labelled it like that to fool his wife. I pointed it out to Gudbjörn. He grabbed the bottle and sniffed it.

'It *is* berry juice,' he said.

'Probably deadly after all these years,' I cautioned. Without a moment's hesitation, he took a robust swig from the bottle. It was typical of him.

'Not a bad nightcap,' he said, sighing gustily.

He took another generous swig.

'If I can't wake you in the morning, I'll know why,' I said.

Gudbjörn laughed, then asked: 'Do you think he made coffins down here?' as if following on directly from my comment.

'No idea,' I said. 'Let's go back upstairs.'

I turned off the light. He brought the book of photos up with him. I was feeling sleepy now and looked forward to hitting my pillow. I said goodnight to Gudbjörn but left my door ajar as I have an aversion to sleeping with the door shut. I switched on the bedside light, which had a fringed shade that cast barred shadows on the yellow walls, and took down a book at random from the shelf. It turned out to be an ancient edition of *Pilgrim's Progress* – not exactly my cup of tea.

'Have you finished with that book?' I called in a low voice through the partition wall. No reply. I sighed and began to leaf through Bunyan. The old concrete house was deathly quiet. I turned off the fringed lamp and closed my eyes. Shortly afterwards I was asleep.

III

I woke up again around midnight. I had been dreaming but couldn't remember what about. Feeling thirsty, I got out of bed, despite my sleep-drugged state. The linoleum was cold underfoot and I instinctively clenched my toes. It was pitch-black in the hallway. I went into the kitchen and the fridge hiccupped into life with a droning hum. It was a big old American model; and there in the kitchen, with the trees clustering thickly at the window, I thought for a moment that I had crossed the Atlantic and could have been somewhere in the Midwest. I opened the fridge and grabbed a bottle of soda water. The light-bulb flashed me indecipherable messages in Morse as I drank from the neck of the bottle, without closing the door.

I heard a soft noise behind me. Assuming Gudbjörn was thirsty too, I turned to hand him the bottle. But it was not him standing in the kitchen doorway: it was a bent old man, holding a small carving axe in one hand. He was wearing a brown woollen jumper and homespun trousers of the same colour. I saw him quite clearly in the flickering glow from the fridge. The head of the carving axe appeared rusty. The man was not looking at me and I realised he had no eyes. I don't know if I felt chilled simply because I was standing in front of the open fridge. I slowly closed the door and with that the presence vanished. The floor felt even colder than before. I tiptoed to the doorway, reached out for the light-switch in the hall and turned it on. Then I opened the door to Gudbjörn's room. He was lying on his side, with the book from the cellar on the chair beside his bed. I put a hand on his shoulder and shook him. He didn't move. I pushed at him again. Then I noticed that he was strangely stiff, as if made of wood.

The Piano Dealer

I had been sent to Düsseldorf by the College of Music to buy four grand pianos on their behalf. I didn't really feel like going but as I am in fact Vice Principal of the school, and no one else wanted to go, I let myself be talked into it. I had never been to Düsseldorf before. When I arrived on the Frankfurt train, I was tired and went straight to my hotel to sleep. It was an old, white building on the banks of the Rhine; if I looked out of my window I could see a strip of muddy water in the half-light. My first glimpse was a disappointment; I had read about this waterway all my life and always wanted to see it, but the dirty flood that I saw from my window was not at all what I had been led to expect.

I dozed off early and slept right through until morning. The bed was comfortable, and there was no din of traffic outside, yet I fancied I could hear the faint murmur of the river, though it did not disturb me. I had rather a bizarre dream. I was standing on Laugavegur in central Reykjavík early in the evening, about to enter the Mál og menning bookshop to browse through composers' biographies, when a small boy came towards me with a book by Arthur Conan Doyle under his arm, the second volume of the Sherlock Holmes stories. Since these had always been my favourite, I asked if he had read the book. He said no, because he had only just bought it. 'Of course,' I said in my dream. 'It does include the Hound of the Baskervilles, doesn't it?' In that instant the boy began to change, metamorphosing into some kind of animal, though not a dog, and limped past me out of the door, with jet-black hide and a strange hump on its back. It had dropped the book. At the same moment, all the lights in the bookshop went out and someone shouted: 'All the power on earth has run out.'

I remembered the dream when I woke up in the morning, and wrote it down, more or less as I have recorded it here. My appointment with the piano dealer was not until after lunch. I ate breakfast, which was exemplary, as one would expect from a German hotel, then went out and strolled down to the river and along the stone parapet. Countless ships and barges were sailing up and down the brown flood. There was nothing poetic about this waterway, as I had imagined, yet it was impressive in its way – a bit like Iceland's Jökulsá á Fjöllum river. The city, on the other hand, I found more charming than I had anticipated. I wandered through its streets and parks until the time came to meet the piano dealer.

He turned out to be a German businessman to his fingertips; stout, with a greying beard and an air of self-confidence, even self-satisfaction, though all was kept within bounds by his innate courtesy.

It did not take us long to come to an informal agreement and we decided to meet again next day to work out the details. I was extremely pleased with the instruments he had for sale, but did not want to seem too eager, assuming that this was how one behaved when doing business. Later I would need to look into transporting the grand pianos to Hamburg and shipping them from there to Iceland.

I spent the remainder of the afternoon visiting music shops and found a handful of CDs. I had the good luck to come across a double album featuring the blues singer Robert Johnson, whose work I used to own on vinyl when I was about twenty, but had given away to a friend and always regretted. This was despite the fact that my life had subsequently been devoted to studying classical music and I had hardly listened to the blues for the last twenty years. Even so, I felt this music was like no other. To be honest, it possessed something that no classical music could aspire to. I bought the album on impulse, in addition to a work by Mahler and a famous version of Beethoven's string quartet. Yet, somehow, finding the Robert Johnson in that German city gave me the greater pleasure. On my return to the hotel, I put the first disc of his album in my portable CD player and cranked up the volume. After listening to a couple of tracks, I opened the mini-bar and poured myself a glass. When I had played both discs repeatedly and pretty near emptied the mini-bar, I headed out and wandered into the nearest pub, which was on a street corner down by the river. The bar seemed to be full of arty types, noisily showing off, and I didn't speak to anyone. I downed several beers there, before wandering back out into the still evening and penetrating deeper into the city. I ended up in a basement dive, where a small band of black musicians was performing. I sat at the table nearest to them. They took a break, and for some reason the singer struck up a conversation with me. He said he had grown up on the banks of the Missouri, adding: 'It sure beats the Rhine.' When he heard where I came from, he said he had visited Iceland once long ago and played at Hotel Saga. He could still remember the name – *Hotel Saga*. I asked him something about Robert Johnson, and he replied: 'Man, you ain't got a *hope* of singing if you don't know Robert Johnson.' I agreed, aware that my question had been foolish. The singer patted me on the shoulder and drained his beer before returning to the stage. I listened and drank.

A fog had descended by the time I emerged into the street towards dawn. It soon became clear that I was completely lost. At first I tried to find the way myself, but ended up in ever more dubious-looking areas which were quite unfamiliar to me. In the end I gave up and ordered a taxi. By now I couldn't even remember the name of my hotel, but the driver managed with patient skill to work out where it was after I had described the surroundings in slurred tones. When I finally staggered into the hotel garden, I noticed a pair of steel-rimmed glasses lying on the pavement outside the entrance. I picked them up and put them on. I could see precisely nothing through them. I put them in my jacket pocket, meaning to hand them in at reception, but had forgotten all about them by the time I got inside, and made straight for my room to sleep it off.

I woke fairly early, despite the heavy night. I felt grim. Robert Johnson himself could hardly have been in a worse state after one of his benders. I reached for the CD player and put on the first disc again. The thought of my appointment with the piano dealer after lunch made me queasy. I went into the bathroom and threw up. Naturally, breakfast was out of the question. I had suddenly become obsessed with the idea of leaving town on the next train. I'd had more than enough of Düsseldorf. That piano dealer, with his greying beard and air of lazy affluence, could go and jump in the lake as far as I was concerned.

What I really wanted was to go to America.

Taking my little suitcase, I caught a taxi straight to the railway station. The fog had not yet lifted.

'I wish one could take a train all the way to America,' I said to the taxi driver in my terrible German. He glanced at me in the rear-view mirror without speaking. I sensed pity in his eyes, and was not sure if he had understood me.

Then I remembered the glasses I had found last night and put them on again. This time I could see perfectly, and even the fog seemed to recede when I looked through them out of the window on my side of the car.

The Stargazer is Always Alone

a

The telescope stood on its tripod, over by the living-room window. There were no curtains. The man who lived there kept the lights off when darkness fell in the evenings and preferred looking through the telescope to turning on the TV. Sometimes he would examine the stars in the sky. Recently, however, he had taken to studying the two-storey house opposite, which was brightly lit as a rule. The ground floor flat had no curtains either, and the living room was lined with bookshelves; as many, it seemed, as he had in his own living room. Increasingly, after finishing his ready-meal in the evenings, he would go to the telescope and point it at the window across the street. If he homed in on the bookshelves, it was not hard to see which books the man opposite, a total stranger, had on his shelves. As he peered through the telescope, a grimace would twitch his face every now and then when he spotted a book that he did not own himself.

'Damn it,' he would mutter, re-adjusting the focus, before training the telescope on another shelf, which also turned out to contain a book he did not have.

'Damn it,' he said again.

He did this night after night, until it came close to an obsession, like so much in his life. He kept spying more books belonging to this stranger who had recently moved in – books that he did not have himself but would have liked to own. Some were virtually impossible to get hold of. In the daytime, when he went to the post office with a letter to his daughter who lived in Vancouver (and therefore much too far away), or to buy a ready-meal for supper, he would occasionally meet the neighbour from across the road, who owned books that he did not have. They never exchanged greetings, and the newcomer showed no interest in becoming acquainted with the stargazer. Presumably he was unaware that he too collected books. Perhaps it was best that way. It was probably a bad idea for two book collectors to get to know each other. It would lead to an inevitable breach of their friendship if one saw a rare book at the other's house and knew for certain that he couldn't have got it from anyone but a mutual acquaintance, who had promised the book to *him*. Under circumstances like that, all friendly feeling would soon evaporate. So it was better thus: that the stargazer should go on standing at his window in the evenings, envying the stranger this and that title, in between looking up at the stars. There he could read the celestial alphabet, and this provided temporary relief for his envy.

b

One evening, unusually, the lights were out in the room opposite. The skies were clear, but the stargazer was in no mood to study the firmament through his telescope. Nor did he want to sit in front of the TV.

'Damn it,' he said, still under his breath, and looked out of the window again to check whether the lights had come on across the road. He felt weighed down by a sense of solitude. He had never before realised quite what it meant to be alone.

Putting on his jacket and shoes, he went out of his flat, into the dark corridor. He did not bother to switch on the light but walked out through the entrance hall and into the garden below his living-room window. The autumn evening was cool and tranquil. Standing on the dark lawn, he raised his eyes to the sky. He was so accustomed to studying it through the telescope that at first he found it a little hard to identify the position of the constellations. The heavenly bodies seemed so remote, seen with the naked eye; scarcely more than dots, like the eyes of wild beasts in a black jungle. He was carried past this dark forest by a powerful current, riding in a little boat on a black river – a boat that was the earth itself.

He gazed up at the sky for a long time, at Orion, his favourite constellation – he didn't know why – with its great stars Rigel and Betelgeuse, then lowered his gaze to the house across the road.

All the lights were still out.

c

Then his gaze fell on his own lawn. Over by the fence he could make out an irregular circle, oddly similar to the cluster of stars. He moved closer to this greyish-white ring and peered at it. Something indefinable seemed to emanate from it, a sensation he sometimes experienced when examining the stars, magnified a thousandfold, through the telescope. It turned out to be mushrooms, a hundred or more together, conspicuous against the black grass. He was seized by joy, almost euphoria, as if he had made an important discovery.

'They're *ink caps*,' he exclaimed aloud. 'Their ink is unsurpassed for drawing maps of the stars.'

Dragging off his jacket, he tied the sleeves together to create a sort of bundle. Then he bent down and began to tear up the ink caps one by one, laying them inside his jacket. He picked them slowly, inspecting each mushroom in turn, holding some up against the starry sky as if to see how they would fit there, before placing these in his jacket as well. He did not stop until he had picked all the mushrooms. Then taking hold of the sleeves, he lifted his jacket. There were no ink caps left on the lawn. He carried the bundle like a basket. Suddenly he felt as if he were returning from a trip to the forest in the sky, and the mushrooms were a pale heap of asteroids. He descended with slow steps, following a path overshadowed by great, black, spreading branches, before eventually disappearing into his house.

Homo Pastoralis

1

I've wanted to come here for a long time – and now here I am, staying in the pale-blue house down there, which you can see from this vantage point on the hill. I enjoy hobbling on my crutches along the red-gravel paths, admiring the colourful little houses with the tall rowan trees in their gardens. At the foot of the settlement is the souvenir shop, selling extraordinary objects that they make here for people like me. One need go no further than a little way up the hill with the windmill (one of a tiny handful in a country where the wind never drops) for a view of the surrounding area: a vast expanse of rolling grassland dotted with patches of marsh, high mountains in the distance, and the odd farm scattered here and there. This place agrees with me. I feel content as I limp back down to the hollow where the village lies. The red-gravel paths are like veins branching between the houses, converging on the heart of the village with its little square and café. I'm heading that way now. Then there are the greenhouses, strangely elevated and unearthly, reminiscent of the great glass domes on a cloud-wreathed planet in solar system L-5.

2

The inhabitants come out of their houses and wave to me. That's how it is every morning. One can almost believe that the place has a milkman; Enid Blyton should have come here on her summer holidays. The guesthouse is first rate; they even have brown eggs like they do in the English countryside. There's nothing more delightful for breakfast than a brown egg.

My room is blue. When I wake up in the morning, I sometimes think of the old historian who went to visit his friend who was vicar at Mývatn, having just read the spiritualist classic *The Blue Island*. The historian passed out drunk during a picnic on the first day, was carried home to the vicarage and laid in a blue bed with blue bedclothes and blue curtains in a blue room, with the blue lake and a blue sky outside, and was left there to sleep it off. When he awoke he let out a terrified yell, convinced that he was dead. But that's not how I feel in the mornings, no, not at all. To me, the blue colour is symbolic of life, the life I have left to live. It will be a better life. I've never felt as good as I do now, since coming out of hospital. Of course, it was best of all when I lay there high on morphine, but I don't have any of that now. Here in the village, with its colourful houses and its rowan trees, I feel *almost* as good as I did on the morphine. Yet (in spite of what I just said) I have to admit that compared to my previous existence, it sometimes occurs to me that my life is no longer the same. This mood doesn't last long, however, and if it descends I can always go back to my room and turn on the television. The news is relentlessly predictable: suicide bombings in Baghdad. Then I know that what I experience here is real. I haven't crossed over to some island in the next world.

3

Using crutches is not so very tiring. They make a comforting sound as they tap on the red gravel, though it is a bit of a struggle to climb up here to the windmill hill.

But anything is possible.

'Good morning,' a middle-aged woman calls to me from

the garden of one of the uppermost houses as I pass by on my way back down to the village.

'Good morning,' I reply. The tone of these simple words – what lies behind them – matters so much. The trees in her garden grow so thickly that you can hardly see the house for all the foliage. It occurs to me that her sitting room must be dark, yet her face is sunny. She asks me how long I'm planning to stay – not prying, but interested. I say I'd like to stay a very long time.

'Then you could have the house over there, beyond the windmill,' she says, pointing over the hillside to a black wooden house with a turf roof.

'Is it for rent?' I ask.

'It's for sale,' she replies.

I ask for more information. By the time I carry on down the path to the guesthouse I have made up my mind. I'm going to buy the black wooden house. Put down roots here, beneath the sails of the windmill, read Cervantes and grow grass on my roof: Kentucky bluegrass, *Poa pratensis*, by choice.

At that moment a black dog runs across my path.

The Dream Glasses

His sight had become so poor that he couldn't even see properly in his dreams any more. He went to see the optician who had prescribed him glasses for his waking life.

'Can't dreams be blurred?' asked the optician, giving him an odd look.

'Not mine,' the man said emphatically.

'I have some ointment to put on one's eyes at bedtime, but I'm not sure it'll do the trick,' the optician said. He hesitated a moment, then reached into a drawer beside him and brought out an ancient-looking pair of spectacles, with a black elastic band to go round one's head. 'These might help,' he said. 'They belonged to my grandfather. He got them from an old spectacles-maker in Rotterdam.'

The man took off his own glasses and put on the pair the optician handed to him. He could see nothing through them. It's probably a good sign, he thought, not to be able to see through them when one's awake.

'Are they for sale?' he asked.

'Unfortunately not,' said the optician. 'They're an heirloom, with great sentimental value for me. But I'll lend them to you for a few nights.'

The man thanked the optician and took the spectacles home to try them out. He watched television that evening, sitting so close to the set that it looked almost as if he wanted to climb inside. His wife lay on the sofa and watched with him until she nodded off over the programmes as usual. After covering her with a blanket, he went into the bedroom where he strained to read the memoirs of Dr A. J. Cronin, who in middle age had developed a great interest in ophthalmology, just as he first experienced the urge to write – as if from a desire to sharpen men's inner and outer vision at one and the same time.

Eventually the man fell asleep wearing the spectacles that had been bought by the optician's grandfather in a back street of Rotterdam, one rainy day long ago. The black elastic was stretched round his head, like a slice of the night. He was at the age when he no longer needed to wake up for work the following morning. He had retired from all office drudgery, which had been bad for his eyes anyway. He did not miss it, although sometimes there was little to do and his wife could never make it through a whole film with him, so he would sit there alone, peering at the TV screen through his thick lenses until late in the night.

He dreamed of a great forest, an endless carpet of pines, seen from the air. A mist hung over the trees, yet he could see them so clearly that he thought he could count their needles. For now it was not a mist that fell over his inner vision but only a mist in the dream itself, and that was quite different.

He soon realised that he was in a plane, flying over that great forest. Beside him in the cockpit was a beautiful young woman who reminded him a little of his wife as she used to be. The woman was steering the plane, but suddenly vanished from his dream. He himself had taken the controls, and lowered the flight over the forest. The mist was dispersing now, and hung on the branches like grey washing. A moment later he was standing on a hill in the forest with the plane flying overhead – clearly the same one as he had been in a second before. He tossed and turned in his sleep, fumbling at the glasses, tugging a little at the black elastic band. He could see the plane's registration number very clearly: D0-UBT. It disappeared into the distance over the sea and he started to walk through the forest. The light was fading slightly, but he could see all the birds with perfect clarity as they fluttered between the tree trunks, and now it transpired that he knew them all by name, although he was no birdwatcher in waking life. He spotted a wren that was almost the same colour as the twilight from which it emerged, and heard its song.

He walked on. The wide forest thinned out strangely, and without warning he found himself in open country, with a vast plain of potato fields extending endlessly in every direction. It was like the countryside around Thykkvabær, and the grasses waved in the summer breeze.

It dawned on him that he must have strayed into his wife's dream, though she was still lying on the sofa in the sitting room. He realised for the first time that no one is truly separate from other people, not even a couple who have lived together for a long time. All dreams join up at the edges, like squares in a patchwork quilt. He picked up the corner of the duvet cover in his sleep and polished the glasses, before continuing his journey to those great potato fields, deeper into the dream of the woman he had known all these years.

The Summerbook

1

He came from a small town called Melville on the east coast
of the United States, not far from Cape Cod, and had rented
a little house down by the sea in the west of Iceland. It was
an old deserted farmhouse, and his intention was to stay there
all summer.

He came alone to begin with; his wife and daughter
were to join him later in the holidays. He had already paid a
brief visit last winter to check out the lie of the land, for he
was an author and wanted to write a book about his stay.
There were no backwaters left in the States to write about;
such crowds of people everywhere, no peace and quiet to be
found. So far he had written three novels and two collections
of short stories that had been published to little acclaim, and
now, tired of fiction, he was keen to write about something
he had experienced first-hand. What put him on the trail was
a short article about Iceland by a fellow American that he had
found on the Net. After that he felt nowhere else would do
for his 'life experiment' but here on the west coast of
Iceland.

He caught the bus to Borgarnes on a wet and windy
spring day. May was half over but the grass in the meadows
was still brown and lifeless, and the landscape looked
somewhat bleak. Nevertheless, he was in good spirits as he
looked out of the bus window. Sitting in front of him were

two French tourists, who he gathered, from his limited knowledge of French, were heading all the way north to the West Fjords. He listened with one ear, but did not attempt to talk to them. Taking out his backpack just before the bus stopped in the village of Borgarnes, he double-checked that he had brought along *The Outermost House* by Henry Beston – the bible of all those who intend to stay for any length of time in a house on a deserted shore. There was little else in his backpack. The other necessities for his stay would arrive later by lorry. Once they had reached the village, he took a taxi out to the Mýrar district. The driver was fat with a big nose and black stubble on his massive double chin; as he sat there gripping the leather-covered steering wheel he looked like a pelican that has fallen on a cactus. He spoke little English, but pointed to the meter every now and then, as if to remind his passenger that this would not be a free ride.

They turned off the main road onto a wet, rutted dirt track that had clearly been taken mainly by tractors that spring. The taxi driver jabbered something in his mother tongue that the American writer did not understand but guessed was probably cursing. When the car pulled up at the house, the driver glanced back at him with rather a disparaging look, as if to say: 'You're not seriously planning to stay here?'

Admittedly, the house was not a welcoming sight on that raw spring day. It was built of unrendered, grey concrete; some of the windows were boarded up and the glass was cracked in others: in short, a dump. He paid the driver and got out. The car crawled away up the track, and he was alone.

He drew a deep breath and stared out at the rough sea that was as grey as the house. Then he reached into his pocket for the key that had been given to him in Reykjavík by the owner of the house. Does one really need to lock up out here? he wondered, as he approached the crumbling steps.

2

The following day he arranged a pile of empty notebooks on the grey oilcloth that covered the rickety kitchen table, and laid a bunch of pencils beside them. He could never write a book unless he wrote it in longhand first, so he had left his computer behind. He would type up all that he had scribbled here in these black notebooks once he was back home in Melville.

The weather was similar to when he arrived yesterday; the sea the same grey, the tussocky field leading down to it bleached as yellow as an old straw mat that has faded on the doorstep.

He sat down at the kitchen table with a chipped cup, sipping the coffee he had made from some instant powder he found in the cupboard. It was probably left over from last year, but tasted okay. He sharpened a pencil with slow deliberation, looking out of the window at the rusty old posts that had once held a washing line. Maybe ragged children's clothes had fluttered there in the morning breeze long ago. But now those posts were like two disused gallows, looming drearily against the stony sky.

He began to write, as if laying a pavement with tiny mosaic tiles; painstakingly building up, word by word, his account of the journey here and the impression made on him by the house and its surroundings. Although he had already been here once before during last winter's reconnoitre, this felt like arriving for the first time. Then everything had been white; even the walls of the house had been plastered by wind-driven snow. He had travelled up from Reykjavík by jeep with the owner, and they had turned back almost as soon as they drove into the yard. Yet he had known instantly that this was where he wanted to conduct his experiment into living at the end of the world.

3

As the days passed, he was drawn ever more often down to the sea to stroll along the shingle strand, watching the birds. The weather had improved and life was quickening all around him. In the evenings he conscientiously recorded all he had seen that day in his notebooks: the behaviour of the seabirds and waders, the passage of the clouds across the sky, the gradual revival of the vegetation, and his longing for his wife and daughter. He sometimes heard from them via his mobile. His wife said she would come at the agreed time, but there was some note in her voice that struck him as strange, although he didn't comment on the fact. He was conscious of some distance, over and above the distance between their phones. His daughter, on the other hand, sounded the same as ever. He asked her how she was getting on at school, whether she was worried about the exams, and whether she was looking forward to coming over. She replied that she was worried about the exams, and that she was looking forward to coming over.

'Good,' he said.

'That I'm worried about the exams?'

'No.'

'It's okay, Dad,' she said, laughing, but he felt she was too far away for him to laugh with her. His eyes wandered around this lonely kitchen on the edge of the world.

4

He had filled a whole notebook, 160 pages, and started on the next. Every evening he read Henry Beston to learn how to write a book like that, and at the same time to focus his mind on how to write a book that was like no other and truly original.

One day he had a visit from the neighbouring farmer,

whom he had met once before when he asked to borrow their phone as his mobile was playing up. The farmer drove into the yard on his green Zetor and honked the horn. The writer rose from the kitchen table, closing his notebook which was labelled on the cover: *John Sears, The Summerbook*.

He went outside.

'Good morning,' the farmer said in Icelandic, as he climbed down from his tractor.

The writer returned the greeting in English.

'Getting on all right here?' the farmer asked, still in Icelandic.

'I'm fine,' the writer replied in English, having caught the gist.

'I just thought I'd check up on you,' the farmer continued, shuffling his feet awkwardly in his muddy boots. His dog remained in the cab of the tractor, staring curiously out through the dirty glass.

'I'm fine,' the writer said again. It didn't occur to him to invite the farmer in. The farmer climbed back into the Zetor, closing the door of the cab. The dog wagged its tail behind the seat and its master raised a hand in parting. The writer climbed the steps to his house and watched the tractor make its slow way up the drive. Then he went inside, sat down at the kitchen table, opened *The Summerbook* and carried on writing with a newly sharpened pencil.

5

He had filled two notebooks with observations and reflections on life and his existence in this remote backwater by the time the day of his wife and daughter's arrival came round. He had called them two evenings ago, and his wife had answered and said they would be coming with the afternoon plane on the agreed day. But he heard again the flatness in her voice, as if her heart was not in it.

'Don't you want to come?' he asked.

'What do you mean?' she retorted, as if hurt.
'Oh, I just thought…'
'Of course I want to come,' she said.
'I'll be seeing you then,' he said.

6

They did not come that evening, nor the following day. He called, and there was a short message on the answerphone, announcing that they had gone to see his mother-in-law in Vermont. It was his daughter who left the message. She added, 'Sorry, Dad,' and then there was nothing more, only silence. He tried to call his mother-in-law. The answerphone was on there too, saying that she couldn't come to the phone right now.

He sat at the table all that day, writing in his notebook. But instead of writing about the here and now: the sea, the birds, the mountains and clouds, he wrote about his marriage. A fifteen-year marriage that had always been on the fragile side, persevered with perhaps largely for their daughter's sake.

Late that evening he went outside in the light summer night, pausing momentarily by the posts of the washing line and trying to picture the threadbare children's clothes that used to flap there long ago; and the children's mother, pegging out the laundry before wearily trailing back to the newly built house. After that, he made his way down to the sea once more to watch the eider ducks and listen to their oohing cries. The waves plashed against the dark shingle. This was the same sea that lapped at the light stones of Melville.

7

The Summerbook grew in length as the summer progressed. The clouds passed to and fro across the sky, the sun shone, the rain poured down, the sea was calm and rough by turns, the grass grew long and the neighbouring farmer came and cut it.

He had finally managed to make contact with his wife who was staying with her mother, along with their daughter. Her voice was still evasive when she said she wanted to think things over and maybe they should take a break. He did not reproach her for failing to join him, merely said: 'Yes, let's think things over. I'll come back in the autumn and we'll see how things stand.'

His luggage had arrived by lorry in a wooden packing case. When he received it in the yard, it occurred to him that the wooden crate looked uncomfortably like a coffin, as if it contained the earthly remains of his previous life. While he was unpacking the box that evening in his cheerless bedroom, this feeling struck him with even more force. Shaking it off, he arranged his dictionaries on a shelf in the kitchen and put away the rest of his belongings in the appropriate places. He had arranged for the neighbouring farmer to pick up provisions for him in Borgarnes on a regular basis. Now he lacked for nothing but the company of the woman who did not want to come, and their daughter.

8

The house-owner came up from Reykjavík. He appeared without warning, saying he had decided to pop in to see if his tenant was doing okay. He had brought along a bottle of whisky. The weather was good that day so they climbed a mountain and admired the panoramic view over the district, seeing how the waves broke on the yellow sand of the beach. The slopes they climbed had been green right up to the belt of rocks below them. They broached the bottle while up on the mountain, and finished it later that evening back at the house where the writer prepared an unusual meal of tinned meat. It was late July and the light nights were beginning to grow dim.

'I'm getting a lot of writing done here,' the author said, taking a drink from his glass, feeling almost as if he should provide the house-owner with a report.

'Show me,' the other said.

He brought out all the notebooks, packed with his scrawl. He did not usually show half-finished writings to any but those he knew very well. His guest flicked through the notebooks, dipping into them here and there.

'Excellent,' he said, handing them back to the author, who sensed that his landlord had not made head or tail of what he had set down on paper. He pretended he didn't mind or hadn't noticed. He remembered what Emerson said – that the reward of a thing well done is having done it, no more. He sensed a gradual clarification of his ideas about how the book would develop when he got home to Melville in the autumn and sat down at his computer to finish it. It occurred to him that he might be alone in the house there as he was here. But somehow that thought had become more bearable than before.

Soon after the whisky was finished, the visitor began to prepare for his return to Reykjavík. He got behind the wheel of his car, despite having drunk at least half a bottle. The writer tried to tell him that he shouldn't go home in that state. He could stay here; there was a mattress he could sleep on. But it didn't matter what he said, his visitor was determined to leave.

'Everyone drink-drives here,' he said, shutting the door, then rolled down his window and called: 'Drop by and see me before you leave at the end of August.' It sounded like an order. Perhaps he was afraid he wouldn't receive his final payment.

The author raised a hand and said of course he would drop round, then went into the house in the dusk. He blew out the candles and got ready for bed. His mind was whirring with countless thoughts, magnified by the alcohol, and he did not fall asleep until dawn.

9

August had arrived. The evenings were drawing in, and the tussocky hayfield had long been mown and begun to grow anew. He had filled five books with unconnected thoughts. Added together it came to 800 pages in under three months. That was almost ten pages a day. He had stopped using the mobile phone, turned it off and packed it in the crate from home. Gradually he was beginning to put things back into the box. Maybe one item a day that he wanted to take home with him. It was like a daily ritual. And then there would be stones from the beach, pebbles, of all different colours, and the skeleton of a bird that he had found, as well as a bunch of wood cranesbill that he had picked and dried for his daughter. Although he still wrote mostly about what passed before his eyes each day, in his mind he had partly returned to the seaside township of Melville, not far from Cape Cod. Thoreau had stayed there and written about Iceland, which he knew of from books. He wondered if Thoreau would have thought it worthwhile coming here, but told himself: 'No, probably not.'

10

It rained the day he left. The posts of the washing line outside the kitchen window had never looked more forlorn. They now resembled nothing but gallows, making it impossible to imagine that children's clothes could ever have hung on a line between them.

The farmer drove over, in a Land Rover this time, not the tractor. The writer had arranged all his notebooks neatly in the top of the wooden crate. It no longer reminded him of a coffin, but of one of those containers for nourishing life in plants or seedlings. He placed Henry Beston's holy writ in the box alongside the notebooks, as well as his dictionaries, clothes and other personal belongings. They carried the box outside and slid it into the back of the Land Rover.

When, sitting in the car with the farmer and his dog, he turned round in the rain to look back at the dark-grey, rain-lashed house, he hardly knew why he had spent so long here, so far away from home. The rectangular packing case lay in the back of the Land Rover, the dog beside it, resting on its paws. The rain drummed on the roof and windscreen of the car. He thought of his wife, of his daughter, of their house in Melville and *The Summerbook* that he meant to complete there that winter while the sea lapped at the light-coloured shingle that was so different from the grey-black stones of this shore.

The Silence Room

Sean O'Brien

ISBN: 978 1905583171
RRP: £7.95

'Sean O'Brien does for libraries what Ursula Andress did for bikinis. Read and rejoice!' - Val McDermid

Chain-smoking alcoholics, warring academics, gothic stalkers and aspiring writers are just some of the visitors that browse the mysterious library at the heart of Sean O'Brien's fiction debut. Idlers and idolisers alike can be referenced, in body or in text, among the crepuscular alcoves and dim staircases of this seemingly unassuming building. The secret to a family curse, a dog-eared first edition of Stevens' Harmonium, the gruesome fate of a feminist literary theorist - all are available to simply take down from the shelf, as are the catalogue of genres and subject areas that O'Brien himself effortlessly deploys: from gothic horror to English pastoral, Critical Theory to Cold War noir.

'Sean O'Brien, like Graham Greene, creates his own instantly recognisable fictional landscape, where crime, mystery and disillusion lurk by the waters of the Tyne or Humber. His stories glint with black comedy and touches of the macabre and surreal. In O'Brien country you may hear the hoot of a train pulling out of the city, but you'll never be on it, because your place is here in the kingdom of backstreet pubs, tired, desirable girls and drowned men. Nothing is ever as it seems: it is much more frightening than that... First-class stories from one of our finest writers.' - Helen Dunmore

Under the Dam
and other stories

DAVID CONSTANTINE

ISBN: 0954828011
RRP: £7.95

'Flawless and unsettling'
Boyd Tonkin, Books of the Year, *The Independent*

'I started reading these stories quietly, and then became obsessed, read them all fast, and started re-reading them again and again. They are gripping tales, but what is startling is the quality of the writing. Every sentence is both unpredictable and exactly what it should be. Reading them is a series of short shocks of (agreeably envious) pleasure.'
- A S Byatt, Book of the Week, *The Guardian*

'A superb collection'- *The Independent*

'This is a haunting collection filled with delicate clarity. Constantine has a sure grasp of the fear and fragility within his characters.'
- A L Kennedy